The Christmas Plan

A Holly Falls Christmas

Judy Powers

Table of Contents

Prologue
Amy - November 26th

Amy Donovan had a system for everything. Laundry. Grocery shopping. Optimized weeknight pasta.

A holiday romance? Not so much.

She had color-coded her entire life, except for the one thing that actually mattered.

The spreadsheet glowed on her laptop screen in the dimming light of her apartment, cursor blinking in the cell labeled "Probability of Success." She'd calculated conversion rates for her consulting firm's biggest mergers. She'd optimized supply chains for Fortune 500 companies. Last year, she'd built a financial model that predicted a market correction three weeks before it happened, saving her client $17 million.

But she couldn't figure out how to stop spending holidays alone.

Outside her window, New York City sparkled with lights strung between buildings, cheerful and relentless. Somewhere fourteen floors below, families were probably still digesting turkey, still laughing over pumpkin pie, still pretending they enjoyed each other's company. She'd told her father and Liz she couldn't get away from work. She'd told her mother the same thing last year, and the year before that.

The lie got easier each time. The truth didn't.

Her phone sat face-down on the granite countertop, three voicemails blinking unheard. She knew what they said. Her mother asking if she was bringing someone special to Christmas. Dawn calling to tell her about some amazing thing she'd seen in Portugal or Prague or wherever her sister had landed this month. Her father, his voice careful and kind, checking in.

She picked up her wine glass. Empty. When had that happened?

The Thanksgiving takeout containers sat in the trash, the fancy ones from the place on Madison that charged forty-seven dollars for a single serving of turkey and all the trimmings. It had tasted like cardboard, but she'd eaten it anyway, sitting at her dining table with her laptop open, working through the holiday like it was any other Friday.

It wasn't any other Friday.

This morning, Jessica from Contracts had stopped by Amy's desk, her left hand extended with theatrical casualness, a diamond catching the fluorescent lights. "Derek proposed last night. Can you believe it? Thanksgiving dinner with his whole family, and he just got down on one knee right there in front of everyone."

Amy had said the right things. Made the right sounds. Hugged Jessica with what she hoped passed for genuine enthusiasm.

Then she'd gone to the bathroom and stared at her reflection for six minutes, she'd timed it, trying to remember the last time someone had looked at her the way Derek apparently looked at Jessica. Like she was the answer to a question he'd been asking his whole life.

Peter had looked at her like she was a project. A problem to be managed.

The memory surfaced before she could stop it. Eight months into their relationship, Peter sitting across from her at the Thai place they went to every Tuesday, his expression patient and pained. "You schedule romance like a board meeting, Amy. I feel like I'm on your calendar, not in your life."

She'd tried to explain. Tried to make him understand that planning wasn't controlling, it was caring. She planned because she wanted things to work. Because she was terrified of the alternative.

He'd paid for dinner and walked her home and ended it on her doorstep with the efficiency of a man checking an unpleasant task off his list.

That was three years ago. She'd dated since then. Six men in three years, each lasting an average of four-point-three months before they invented increasingly creative excuses to exit her life.

"So, what do you do for fun?" She'd tilted her head, trying for casual interest instead of a job interview. "Me? Oh, you know. Reading. Hiking. I'm very spontaneous." She'd attempted a laugh that came out like a cough. "I mean, not too spontaneous. I have a calendar. But I'm flexible about the calendar. Sometimes." She'd leaned closer to the mirror and lowered her voice. "Do you like books?" she'd asked the mirror. "Me too. Everyone does. Right?" Her smile had twitched. "Unless you don't. Which is also fine. Totally fine. We could do something else. I'm open to suggestions. Within reason. Safety first." She'd caught sight of her own desperate expression and wanted to crawl under the sink.

The bathroom door swung open.

Amy's head snapped up. Jessica stood frozen in the doorway, one hand still on the handle, her engagement ring catching the light.

"Oh," Jessica said. "I didn't realize anyone was… "

"I wasn't." Amy straightened, turned on the tap for no reason. "Just checking my… "

"Were you practicing?" Jessica's perfectly shaped eyebrows lifted. "In the mirror?"

"No."

"Because it looked like you were having a conversation with yourself. Something about hobbies and weekend plans?"

Amy's face burned. She had been practicing. Rehearsing casual conversation openers because apparently she needed a script for basic human interaction. "I was just thinking out loud."

"Right." Jessica's expression shifted from surprise to something worse, pity. "You know, Derek has a friend. We could set up a… "

"I'm fine."

"Amy… "

"Congratulations on your engagement." Amy grabbed a paper towel she didn't need. "The ring is beautiful. Derek's a lucky guy."

She walked out before Jessica could finish whatever well-meaning, terrible thing she'd been about to say.

Back at her desk, Amy opened her laptop.

The spreadsheet was already there, created two days ago in a moment of wine-soaked clarity that now felt more like madness. But she hadn't deleted it. Hadn't closed the file. Instead, she'd spent the last forty-eight hours filling it in, justifying it, perfecting it.

PROJECT: CHRISTMAS HUSBAND

The title looked desperate. It was desperate. She was desperate and twenty-nine years old with a corner office and no one to call when her mother left voicemails asking if she was bringing someone special home for the holidays.

The spreadsheet had seven tabs. Seven. Because if she was going to do this, she was going to do it properly. Still, it took a few minutes to start reading her entries.

Tab 1: OBJECTIVE & SUCCESS METRICS

Primary Objective: Secure suitable long-term partner (marriage potential) before December 25th.

Success Criteria:

- Mutual attraction (verified through minimum three dates)
- Compatible values (assessment questionnaire developed)
- Long-term potential (financial stability, career trajectory, family orientation)
- Family approval (introduced by December 24th)
- Risk Mitigation: Build in 15% buffer for cancellations, 20% contingency for personality misalignment

Tab 2: TARGET LOCATION ANALYSIS

Holly Falls, Vermont

- Population: 3,847
- Median age: 34
- Male/female ratio: 1.08:1
- Median income: $62,000
- Preliminary assessment: Above-average ratio of single males in target demographic (28-38)
- Strategic advantage: Sister Dawn currently residing in location; provides built-in social proof and community access

Tab 3: CANDIDATE DATABASE

This was the tab that made her stomach hurt. Seventeen names, pulled from social media deep-dives, Dawn's casual mentions, and one very productive hour spent combing through the Pleasant Valley Herald's online archives.

1. Michael Donovan, 32, CPA Strengths: Stable career, owns home, active in community theater Weaknesses: TBD

(requires field assessment) Compatibility Probability (Preliminary): 67% Status: RESEARCH PHASE

2. David Patterson, 29, Bookstore Owner Strengths: Creative field, community ties, reads literary fiction Weaknesses: Divorced (amicable per public records), may have commitment issues Compatibility Probability (Preliminary): 71% Status: RESEARCH PHASE

3. Christopher Lyle, 35, High School Teacher Strengths: Stable employment, pension plan, coaches basketball Weaknesses: Still lives with mother (temporary per Dawn's intel) Compatibility Probability (Preliminary): 58% Status: RESEARCH PHASE

4. William Crane, 32, Historian/Business Owner Strengths: Local ties (family business), intelligent (verified: Master's degree), good with hands (verified via observation of shelf repair in background of town hall photo) Weaknesses: Excessive cynicism re: holiday traditions (per Dawn: "total Grinch"), resistance to planning, appears commitment-averse based on seven-year gap since last known relationship Compatibility Probability (Preliminary): 63% Status: RESEARCH PHASE Notes: Owns antique shop on Main Street. Town historian. Appears in 12 community event photos over past two years. Strong jawline. Irrelevant but notable.

She'd continued through all seventeen. Some entries were more complete than others. Some she'd added just to reach a statistically significant sample size.

Tab 4: ENGAGEMENT STRATEGY

Phase 1 (Dec 1-7): Initial Contact & Assessment
- *Attend minimum 5 community events*
- *Initiate casual conversation with top 8 candidates*

- *Narrow field to top 5 based on in-person chemistry assessment*

Phase 2 (Dec 8-14): Active Pursuit

- *Schedule individual interactions with top 3 candidates*
- *Deploy strategic vulnerability (controlled disclosure of personal information)*
- *First kiss target date: December 14 (statistically optimal for pre-Christmas romance)*

Phase 3 (Dec 15-21): Relationship Acceleration

- *Select primary candidate*
- *Introduce to family context*
- *Secure commitment indicator (exclusivity agreement minimum)*

Phase 4 (Dec 22-25): Consolidation

- *Bring candidate home for Christmas*
- *Achieve family approval*
- *Establish post-holiday relationship trajectory*

Tab 5: CONTINGENCY PLANNING

Tab 6: BUDGET & RESOURCES

Tab 7: DAILY SCHEDULE & ACTIVITY LOG

She scrolled back to the candidate list. Stared at William Crane's entry. That detail about his jawline, why had she written that? It wasn't relevant. It wasn't part of any reasonable assessment criteria.

She highlighted the sentence. Her finger hovered over the delete key.

She closed the laptop instead.

The apartment pressed in around her. Immaculate countertops. Dish towel folded in precise thirds. Every appliance exactly where it should be.

She'd organized her spice rack alphabetically last weekend. She'd color-coded her closet by season and garment type. Her life was perfect.

Her life was suffocating.

She opened her laptop again. Navigated to the travel booking site she'd already pulled up six times in the past two days.

Flight Search: NYC (JFK) to Burlington, VT Departure: December 1 Return: December 26

The cursor blinked in the search box, patient as a therapist.

She thought about Jessica's ring. About Peter's face when he'd told her that being with her felt like dating a life coach who'd forgotten to clock out. About Thanksgiving dinner alone with her laptop and forty-seven dollars' worth of someone else's idea of tradition.

She thought about her mother's voice on the voicemail she hadn't listened to yet, asking the same question she asked every year. Hoping for a different answer.

She thought about the spreadsheet. About seventeen strangers who didn't know they'd been catalogued, assessed, and assigned probability scores. About the tab labeled **CONTINGENCY PLANNING** that she'd filled with backup strategies and risk mitigation protocols.

About the fact that she'd been working on this document for forty-eight hours and hadn't questioned the fundamental insanity of it until just now.

Her phone buzzed. Text from Dawn: *Mom called me asking about you. You okay? Please tell me you didn't work through Thanksgiving. Come to Holly Falls for Christmas. I'm staying through New Year. It'll be fun. We can be pathetic together.*

Amy's throat tightened. Dawn didn't know about the spreadsheet. Dawn didn't know that Amy had already researched the population demographics of her sister's current location like she was planning a military campaign.

Dawn thought Amy was just visiting.

She typed back: *I'm fine. And yes, coming for Christmas. Can't wait to see you.*

Then she opened the spreadsheet one more time. Read through the entries. The strategies. The timeline that would take her from arrival to coupled-up in twenty-five days.

It was insane. It was also the only plan she had.

She pulled up the flight booking site and entered her credit card information before she could change her mind. The confirmation email arrived thirty seconds later.

Confirmation: Flight AA4792, December 1, 6:45 AM departure.

She saved the spreadsheet to the cloud drive. Created a backup on her external hard drive. Synced it to her phone.

Then she poured herself another glass of wine and stood at her window, looking out at the city that held eight million people and somehow couldn't produce one who wanted to love the girl who folded her dish towels in precise thirds.

Tomorrow she would pack. She would select her most strategically festive wardrobe items. She would print out her research and her schedules and her contingency plans.

Tonight, she would sit with the terrifying possibility that no amount of planning would ever be enough.

The cursor blinked on her screen.

She clicked save one more time.

Just to be sure.

Chapter 1
Amy - December 1st

Amy's carefully curated life had not prepared her for Holly Falls in December.

The town looked like someone had given a Victorian postcard unlimited access to every craft store in New England and absolutely no adult supervision. Wreaths hung from every lamppost. Garland wrapped around every tree trunk. The storefronts weren't decorated so much as aggressively festooned, each window trying to out-Christmas its neighbor with increasingly alarming enthusiasm.

And the noise.

She'd forgotten about small-town noise. Not traffic noise, she could handle traffic. This was worse. This was children shrieking in the town square, their voices bouncing off the brick buildings. This was someone's sound system blasting "Jingle Bell Rock" at a volume that suggested the speaker was trying to communicate with passing aircraft. This was a dozen conversations happening simultaneously within a fifteen-foot radius, everyone knowing everyone, everyone shouting greetings across the square like they couldn't simply text like civilized people.

Amy stood beside her rental car, trying to remember how to breathe.

In New York, she could walk ten blocks and encounter maybe one person she knew, if she was lucky. Here, she'd been parked for ninety seconds and had already been waved at twice by strangers who apparently thought friendly acknowledgment was mandatory.

Her fingers found her phone. She pulled up her schedule, color-coded, cross-referenced, synced across two devices. Seeing the day laid out in orderly blocks made her lungs work properly again.

9:47 AM: Arrive Holly Falls

10:00 AM: Check in Evergreen Lodge

10:30 AM: Unpack, organize clothing by category and occasion

11:15 AM: Review candidate profiles

12:00 PM: Lunch at Main Street Diner (reconnaissance)

She was ahead of schedule. Thirteen minutes ahead, which should have felt good but instead felt destabilizing. Early meant unstructured time. Unstructured time meant improvisation. Improvisation meant chaos.

She could walk to the lodge. It was only two blocks according to her map, and walking would eat up seven of those thirteen minutes. That would put her at 9:54, which was much closer to the planned arrival time and therefore more acceptable.

Decision made, she locked the car and started across the town square, phone in hand, GPS open even though she could literally see her destination from here. But the blue dot on the screen was comforting. The turn-by-turn directions were comforting. The little notification that said "Arrive in 4 minutes" was—

Her heel caught.

Not a dramatic catch. Not a twist-your-ankle, fall-on-your-face catch. Just enough of a snag on the uneven cobblestone to make her stumble forward, arms windmilling slightly, phone sailing from her grip.

Her phone sailed out of her hand and into a storm drain with all the grace of her rapidly unraveling morning.

She heard the splash before she registered what had happened.

She stared as her GPS arrow spun in soggy circles. Her color-coded schedule, gone. Her carefully timed arrival plan, wrecked. Her dignity, scraped somewhere on the cobblestones of Holly Falls.

Directly in front of her, a man crouched over the cobblestones with what looked like a very expensive camera. He had a photograph in one hand, old, sepia-toned, the edges soft with age. A cup of coffee sat on the stones beside him.

Well… had sat on the stones beside him.

Now the cup was on its side, dark liquid spreading across the cobblestones in an accusatory puddle, and Amy's forward momentum was carrying her directly into his personal space.

He looked up.

She grabbed his shoulder to stop herself from actually trampling him.

His hand shot out and caught her elbow, steadying her with surprising gentleness for someone whose coffee she'd just murdered.

They froze like that. Her hand on his shoulder. His hand on her elbow. Both of them staring at the photograph, which now had three drops of coffee speckling its surface like terrible freckles.

"I am so sorry." The words came out in a rush. "I didn't see you. I was just—my phone—"

"You're standing on a historical landmark." His voice was deep and measured, with the particular patience of someone who was definitely not feeling patient.

She looked down. Her heel had caught in the gap between two cobblestones. Old cobblestones. Very old, probably. The kind that people who cared about history got excited about.

"I'm standing on the sidewalk."

"This sidewalk was installed in 1887 using stones imported from—"
He stopped. Blinked. Looked past her shoulder. "Did something just fall?"

They both turned.

Her phone lay face-up in the storm drain, its screen still glowing, the
GPS arrow spinning in confused circles as it tried to orient itself six inches
underwater.

"No." The word came out flat. "No, no, no."

Amy dropped to her knees beside the grate. The phone was right there.
Right there. She could see it. But the openings in the grate were too narrow
for her hand, and the phone was just far enough down that her fingers
couldn't reach.

"Do you have a—" She looked up at the man, who had risen to his
feet and was now staring down at her with an expression somewhere
between concern and exasperation. "Do you have something I could use
to—"

"To fish your phone out of the municipal drain?"

"Yes."

"No." He crouched beside her anyway, peered down at the phone.
"That's not good."

"I'm aware."

"Backed up to the cloud?"

"Yes, but—" But the cloud wasn't in her hand. The cloud didn't have
her schedule with the color-coded blocks that kept her day from dissolving
into chaos. The cloud wasn't in her hand. It didn't vibrate every thirty
minutes to nudge her like a digital conscience.

She sat back on her heels. Stared at the phone's glowing screen as it
flickered and died.

Thirteen minutes ahead of schedule had just become a complete schedule catastrophe.

"I'm sorry about your coffee," she said, because she needed to say something and all the other words trying to escape were variations on screaming.

"It was terrible coffee anyway." He stood, offered her a hand up.

She looked at the hand. Large. Calloused in a way that suggested actual manual labor, not a gym membership. There was a thin scar across his knuckles.

She took it. Let him pull her to her feet.

He was tall. That was her first coherent thought once she was vertical. Tall enough that she had to look up despite her three-inch heels, which meant he was probably six-two, maybe six-three. Dark hair that needed a trim, silver threading the temples in a way that suggested either premature graying or excellent genetics. Blue eyes, very blue, the kind of blue that would photograph well, not that she was thinking about photographing him, that would be insane.

A small scar cut through his left eyebrow.

She was staring. She was absolutely staring.

"You're bleeding." He nodded at her knee.

She looked down. A small scrape, nothing serious, blood beading in a thin line. She hadn't even felt it happen.

"I'm fine."

"You should clean that."

"I'm fine," she repeated, then immediately felt like an idiot because she very clearly wasn't fine. Her phone had drowned in stormwater, her schedule was gone, and she'd just destroyed this man's coffee and possibly damaged what looked like an irreplaceable historical photograph.

"The picture." She pointed at it, still clutched in his hand. "Is it ruined?"

He held it up to the light. The three coffee drops had already started to seep into the paper, creating dark halos. "Probably."

"Can it be restored?"

"Maybe. If I can find someone who knows how to work with nineteenth-century albumen prints without destroying them completely."

She didn't know what an albumen print was, but she understood expensive and irreplaceable when she heard it. "I'll pay for the restoration."

"You don't need to—"

"I absolutely need to. I destroyed your property. That makes it my responsibility."

Something shifted in his expression. Not quite a smile. More like he was reassessing her and wasn't sure what he was seeing. "The photograph was documenting these cobblestones. I was cataloging the wear patterns for the historical society's records."

"You were photographing the sidewalk?"

"Historical sidewalk."

"It's still a sidewalk."

"And your phone was worth retrieving from a storm drain."

She opened her mouth. Closed it. He had a point.

"What's in the picture?" She nodded at the photograph in his hand.

He held it out. She stepped closer, too close, probably, but she wanted to see what she'd ruined.

The photograph showed an ornate box sitting in what looked like this very square. The box was maybe three feet tall, covered in elaborate metalwork, with what appeared to be a large, decorative lock on the front.

"The Wish Box," he said. "This was taken in 1924, the last time it was photographed before being moved to its current location."

"Current location being?"

He pointed over her shoulder.

She turned. There, maybe twenty feet away, surrounded by a decorative iron fence and absolutely drowning in Christmas lights, sat the box from the photograph. Larger than she'd expected. More elaborate. The metalwork caught the morning sun, throwing intricate shadows across the cobblestones.

"That's been there the whole time?"

"Since 1887. Same year as these cobblestones you were standing on."

"You really care about cobblestones."

"I care about history."

"Even the boring parts?"

"Especially the boring parts. That's where the real stories are."

Before Amy could formulate a response to that, because what kind of response did you give to someone who found cobblestones fascinating, a woman's voice rang out across the square.

"William! There you are!"

They both turned.

A woman in a red coat bustled toward them, bells, actual bells, jingling on her sleeves. She was maybe fifty, with short gray hair and the kind of energetic smile that suggested she ran on pure enthusiasm and possibly caffeine.

"Karen." William's tone was carefully neutral. "Good morning."

"It is a good morning. A wonderful morning." She reached them, slightly breathless, and immediately turned that high-wattage smile on Amy. "And you must be Amy Donovan. Dawn's sister. She said you were arriving today."

Amy blinked. "How did you—"

"Small town, dear. We know everything. Well, not everything. But most things. The important things." She thrust out a hand. "Karen Posey. Mayor of Holly Falls. Welcome, welcome. Are you settling in all right? Do you need anything? Directions? Restaurant recommendations? An eligible bachelor?"

"I—what?"

"Nothing." William said the word quickly. "She doesn't need anything."

"Of course she does. Everyone needs something." Karen beamed at both of them. "And isn't this perfect? Just perfect. You've already met William."

"Met is a strong word," Amy said.

"I tripped her and made her drop her phone in the city drain," William added.

"I spilled coffee on his photograph."

"And now you're talking." Karen clapped her hands together. "Wonderful. This is going to work out beautifully."

Amy felt the conversation slipping out of her control. "What's going to work out?"

"The Wish Box project, of course." Karen gestured at the ornate box behind its fence. "Every year we have a new display, a new story about the history and the legend. This year, we're doing something special for the Christmas gala fundraiser. We need someone to research the history, that's William, he's our town historian, and someone to help organize and present the findings. That's you."

"That's not me."

"Of course it is. Dawn mentioned you're a consultant. You organize things. You present things. You make things work efficiently." Karen's smile never wavered. "And you'll be here through Christmas anyway, so you might as well have something to do besides just visiting family."

"I have things to do."

"Wonderful. Then you can add this to your list. The gala is on December twenty-fourth. That gives you plenty of time."

"I don't think—"

"William will fill you in on all the details. Won't you, William?"

William looked like a man who'd just watched his peaceful morning dissolve into chaos and couldn't figure out how it had happened. "Karen, I don't think we need—"

"Of course you do. The grant committee specifically requested a comprehensive presentation. You can't do it alone." She patted his arm. "And now you don't have to. See? Everything works out." She checked her watch. "Oh, I have a meeting with the superintendent in ten minutes. Amy, you're staying at the Evergreen Lodge, yes? It's just over there." She pointed at the sprawling Victorian painted in what could only be described as aggressively festive green. "Two blocks. You can't miss it."

"I can see it from here."

"Perfect. Then you don't need directions. William, be a dear and help her get settled. She's had a rough morning." With a final jingle of bells, Karen Posey bustled away, leaving Amy and William standing beside a puddle of coffee and a storm drain that had swallowed her entire schedule.

William cleared his throat. "I should apologize. Karen means well, but she's—"

"Impossible to say no to?"

"I was going to say enthusiastic, but yes."

Amy looked at the Wish Box. At the photograph in William's hand. At the storm drain where her phone had met its untimely end.

This was not part of the plan. Working on some historical project with a man who cared deeply about cobblestones was not on any of her spreadsheets. She was supposed to check in, unpack, review her candidate profiles, and begin Phase One of her carefully constructed strategy.

Instead, she was standing in a town square that looked like Christmas had vomited on it, bleeding from her knee, phoneless, and apparently volunteered for a project she hadn't agreed to.

"I didn't say yes," she pointed out.

"I noticed."

"So technically, I'm not obligated to help with this Wish Box thing."

"Technically, no."

"But she's going to keep asking."

"Relentlessly." He looked at her with something that might have been sympathy. "She once convinced a retired couple from Boston to chair the Fourth of July committee. They were here for a three-day weekend. They ended up buying a house."

Amy's laugh surprised them both. It came out short and startled, like she'd forgotten how laughing worked.

William's mouth twitched. Almost a smile.

"You really care about that box," she said.

"The Wish Box has been part of this town since 1887. There's a legend attached to it. A history. It matters."

"Even though you can't open it?"

"Because we can't open it. That's what makes it interesting."

She should walk away. Thank him for steadying her after her stumble, apologize again for the coffee and the photograph, and walk directly to the Evergreen Lodge where she could buy a new phone and rebuild her schedule and get back to the plan.

Instead, she heard herself say, "What's the legend?"

His expression shifted. For the first time since their collision, he looked genuinely interested rather than resigned. "The box grants wishes. But only to those who prove themselves worthy."

"Worthy how?"

"That's the question, isn't it?" He gestured at the box with the photograph. "It hasn't been opened in a hundred years. People have tried. Locksmiths. Historians. One very determined woman with a blowtorch in 1973."

"What happened?"

"The lock melted. The box didn't open. She's still bitter about it."

Amy studied the box. From here, she could see the lock, intricate, beautiful, completely unyielding. "So it's just decoration. A tourist attraction."

"Maybe. Or maybe the legend is true and no one's been worthy yet."

"Do you believe that?"

He was quiet for a moment. "I believe this town needs its stories. And I believe some things are worth preserving even if they don't make logical sense."

She looked at him. In the careful way he held the damaged photograph. At the coffee stain spreading across his shirt sleeve that he hadn't mentioned once.

At the way he was looking at the Wish Box like it mattered.

Her phone buzzed in her pocket.

Except her phone was dead in a storm drain.

She reached for it anyway, muscle memory, and found nothing.

The panic hit fresh. Twenty-three days until Christmas. Seventeen candidates on her spreadsheet. A detailed timeline that required precise execution. And no phone.

"I need to go." She took a step back. "I need to buy a phone. And clean this scrape. And check in. And—"

"The Evergreen Lodge is two blocks that way." He pointed. "There's a phone store on Main Street, three blocks past the lodge."

"Thank you."

"And Amy?" He waited until she looked at him. "The photograph will be fine. It's survived worse."

She nodded. Started to walk away. Stopped.

"I didn't agree to help with the Wish Box thing."

"I know."

"So don't expect me to show up and start researching wish-granting boxes."

"I won't."

"Good."

She made it five steps before his voice stopped her again.

"The historical society meets tomorrow night. Seven o'clock at the town hall. If you change your mind."

She didn't turn around. "I won't."

"Just in case."

She walked away, very aware that he was watching her go, very aware that her heel kept catching on the historical cobblestones, very aware that she'd just had a thirteen-minute conversation with a man who wasn't on her spreadsheet and had somehow ended up more interesting than any of the seventeen who were.

The Evergreen Lodge loomed ahead, painted in that aggressive green, and Amy Donovan, who had color-coded her entire life, tried very hard not to think about the fact that her carefully constructed plan was already falling apart.

And she'd only been in Holly Falls for seventeen minutes.

Chapter 2
William - December 1st

William Crane liked things that stayed where they were put.

Antique books with cracked spines. Brass instruments pointed at stars long since forgotten. Town ledgers from 1847, where property disputes were recorded in precise cursive.

Everything in his shop obeyed a kind of order, unspoken, reliable, unlike the dreams of women that involved law firms and capital cities.

He adjusted the lamp and studied the damaged photograph. It was salvageable, unlike the relationship that had ended with blocked numbers and the word "slumming" flung like a grenade.

Three years since Ava left. Three years since he'd let anyone past the polite barrier of small-town cordiality.

And now there was Amy Donovan, with her calendars and crisis planning and the kind of determined energy that ruined perfectly good routines.

He didn't want curious.

Curious got you coffee-stained photographs and the echo of doors closing behind smart women with smarter ambitions.

William's hand froze above the photograph.

Three drops of coffee bloomed across the century-old paper like inkblots, soaking into the image of the Christmas Wish Box he'd been documenting.

He hated this feeling. The sharp awareness. The pull.

He'd spent three years avoiding exactly this, the moment when someone new became someone noticed. Three years of careful restoration work, of predictably cataloged objects and reliable routines. Nothing in his carefully ordered life left coffee stains on his equilibrium.

Until today.

The Wish Box stared up at him from the damaged photograph, blurred behind the spreading disaster. Some things were meant to endure. Others never had a chance.

He carefully blotted the coffee, assessing the damage. Salvageable. Unlike some things. Unlike the relationship that had ended with a woman looking at him with something close to pity and saying his life "doesn't go anywhere."

The photograph would survive with the right treatment. It always did. History was patient that way, willing to wait for someone who cared enough to preserve it.

Unlike people.

He carried the photograph back to his shop, the antique store that had been in his family for three generations. The bell above the door chimed as he entered, that same brass bell his grandfather had installed in 1962, the one that announced every customer, every intrusion into the careful world William had built.

Inside, everything was exactly as it should be. Weathered wood shelves lined the walls, packed with leather-bound books whose gilt titles had faded to whispers. A brass telescope pointed toward a window that overlooked Main Street. An old Victrola sat silent in the corner, waiting for someone to remember how music used to require patience.

This was his territory. His refuge. Every object here had a history, a story, a reason for enduring.

He set the photograph on his restoration table and turned on the lamp. The damage looked worse under direct light; the coffee had seeped deeper than he'd thought, obscuring details he'd been trying to capture.

Just like Ava's departure had obscured his belief that maybe some things could last.

The thought arrived unbidden, unwelcome. Three years should have been long enough to stop making those connections. Three years should have dulled the edge of discovering that the woman you thought understood your commitment to preservation had actually been waiting for you to evolve into something else entirely.

She'd loved the idea of him for exactly six months, loved telling her DC friends about her "small-town historian boyfriend" who lived above an antique shop and knew the provenance of every building in Holly Falls. It made for good stories at gallery openings and cocktail parties.

Then the job offer came. The real job, as she'd called it. The one in DC with the lobbying firm and the corner office and the future that didn't include antique shops or small towns or men who thought preserving the past mattered more than chasing the future.

"Real life has direction," she'd said that last night, her hand sweeping over his shop, the town beyond. "This doesn't go anywhere."

She'd left for DC three weeks later. Blocked his number two weeks after that. He'd heard through mutual friends that she'd described her time in Holly Falls as "slumming it" for the Instagram aesthetic.

That had been the part that hollowed him out. Not the leaving, people left small towns all the time, drawn by bigger opportunities and brighter lights. But the revelation that she'd never actually seen him. Just the character she could play opposite for a while.

He refocused on the photograph. The Wish Box. The town's oldest legend. The thing that had brought Amy Donovan to Holly Falls in the first place, according to the Mayor's enthusiastic introduction at the Bean Counter this morning.

The bell above his door chimed.

William looked up to find Mrs. Childers from the flower shop, holding a small vase.

"William, dear. I found this in my grandmother's attic. Do you think it's worth anything?"

He took the vase and examined it carefully. Early 1900s, hand-painted, minor chips, but structurally sound. "It's lovely. Probably worth about fifty dollars to the right collector."

"Oh, wonderful! Would you be willing to sell it in your shop? I'll split whatever you get for it."

"Of course. I'll add it to the display case."

She beamed, thanked him three times, and left with the particular energy of someone who'd just discovered unexpected value in something they'd thought was worthless.

William placed the vase carefully on his restoration table, made a note to research comparable pieces, and returned his attention to the damaged photograph.

That's when Brad appeared in the doorway, arms crossed, grinning like he knew something William didn't.

Bradley Charles Vane IV, heir to the HomeMakers empire, William's closest friend since third grade, and the only person in Holly Falls who could afford to be bored enough to meddle in other people's business.

"You're scowling at that photograph like it personally offended you," Brad said, walking in without invitation. "What'd it do? Refuse to age gracefully?"

"Someone spilled coffee on it."

"Tragic." Brad picked up the brass telescope, peered through it at nothing. "I hear the Mayor's recruited you for the Wish Box project."

"She mentioned it."

"She mentioned it, or she ambushed you with a visiting consultant and a town-wide mandate?"

William set down his restoration tools. "The latter."

"Thought so. I saw Amy Donovan at the Bean Counter this morning, she was talking about it. Looks like the kind of woman who color-codes her socks. I think everything she had on matched."

"She has a spreadsheet for her coffee order."

"Of course she does." Brad grinned. "You're going to hate working with her."

"I'm going to tolerate working with her. There's a difference."

"Is there?" Brad set down the telescope, studied William with the particular focus of someone who'd known him long enough to read subtext. "You seemed pretty focused on tolerating her when you were staring at her across the square just now."

"I wasn't staring. I was observing."

"You were staring. The way you stare at documents that don't quite add up. Like she's a historical inconsistency you need to solve."

William returned his attention to the photograph. "She spilled coffee on a century-old image and didn't apologize. That's not an inconsistency. That's just carelessness."

"Or she was flustered because you make that face."

"What face?"

"The face that says 'I'm cataloging your flaws for future reference.'" Brad headed for the door. "I'm going to the tree lighting. You coming?"

"I'm obligated to attend as town historian."

"So that's a yes with extra words attached. Good. Maybe you can glare at Amy some more and convince yourself it's professional interest."

Brad left, the bell chiming his exit, and William sat alone with his damaged photograph and the uncomfortable awareness that his best friend was more perceptive than convenient.

He wasn't interested in Amy Donovan. He was cautious around her. There was a difference.

She represented everything he'd learned to recognize as temporary, the kind of energy that swept through small towns taking photographs and making plans and then disappeared back to wherever people like her actually lived. New York, probably. Somewhere with buildings that touched the sky and restaurants that required reservations three months in advance.

She'd be here for what, a few weeks? Long enough to solve the Wish Box mystery for her consulting portfolio or her travel blog or whatever drove people to visit Holly Falls and pretend they understood its history.

Then she'd leave. They always left.

He was just being realistic. Practical. Protecting himself from the inevitable.

At six-thirty, he locked up the shop, pocketed his keys, and walked to the town square for the tree lighting ceremony. Holly Falls transformed in December, every storefront strung with lights, every lamppost wrapped with garland, the air sharp with cold and pine and the particular anticipation that came with the season.

William had complicated feelings about Christmas. Too much forced cheer, too much commercial excess dressed up as tradition. But the tree lighting was different. It was one of the town's oldest customs, dating back to 1887, and even he couldn't deny the magic of watching the massive spruce illuminate against the winter darkness.

The square was packed. Families clustered together, children perched on shoulders, thermoses of hot chocolate passing between cold hands. William found his usual spot, near the historical marker that explained the town's founding, far enough from the crowd to observe without being consumed by it.

That's when he saw her.

Amy Donovan stood near the front, clipboard abandoned for once, her attention completely captured by the tree. The late afternoon sun caught her profile, and William found himself noticing details he'd tried to ignore earlier.

The way she stood, shoulders back, chin lifted, like someone determined to take up exactly the space she occupied. The way her hair fell just below her shoulders, catching the light. The way her expression had softened from the sharp efficiency he'd seen this morning into something that looked almost like wonder.

She was talking to someone, a woman with wild honey-colored hair who had to be the sister the Mayor had mentioned. Dawn, the free spirit to Amy's structure. They were laughing about something, and William watched Amy's guard drop completely for those few seconds.

That's when he made a critical mistake.

He wondered what she looked like when she laughed like that all the time. When she wasn't armed with clipboards and schedules. When she was just... present.

The thought arrived before he could stop it, and he immediately wanted to take it back. To un-notice her. To return to the safe distance of professional obligation.

Too late.

Mayor Karen spotted him from across the square, waved with the enthusiasm of someone who'd just found the solution to a problem. She grabbed Amy's arm, pulling her through the crowd toward William with the particular determination of a small-town mayor on a mission.

"William! There you are! I was just telling Amy about you. Amy Donovan, this is William Crane, our town historian and the only person who actually understands the Wish Box legend well enough to help solve it."

Amy extended her hand, professional and polite. "We met briefly this morning. I'm sorry again about the picture."

"It's salvageable." He shook her hand, noticed it was warmer than expected. Noticed and wished he hadn't.

"I'm glad to hear it. I felt terrible." Her hazel eyes were direct, assessing. "The Mayor mentioned you'd be helping with the Wish Box project?"

"Apparently."

"I promise to be less clumsy around historical artifacts going forward."

"That would be appreciated."

Karen beamed, oblivious to or deliberately ignoring the polite distance in their exchange. "Perfect! You two will work so well together.

Amy's got the organizational skills, William's got the historical knowledge. The Wish Box doesn't stand a chance!"

She bustled away before either of them could protest, leaving William and Amy standing awkwardly in the crowded square.

"She's very enthusiastic," Amy said finally.

"That's one word for it."

"Do you have another?"

"Relentless."

Amy's mouth twitched, not quite a smile, but close. "I can work with relentless. I'm fairly relentless myself."

"I noticed."

"Is that disapproval I'm hearing, or just general wariness of outsiders?"

"It's an observation. You've been in town for six hours and you've already networked with half the business owners and created what I'm guessing is a comprehensive project timeline."

"Seven hours. And it's not comprehensive yet. I'm still gathering data." She tilted her head, studied him with the same assessing look she'd given the town square earlier. "You don't think the Wish Box can be opened, do you?"

"I think it's been locked for twenty-five years and countless people smarter than us have tried."

"So that's a no."

"That's a realistic assessment of the odds."

"And yet you're helping anyway."

"The Mayor is persistent. And the town's history matters, even when it's wrapped in legend."

"Fair enough." She reached for her phone, then remembered she still had to replace it. "I should go. I promised my sister I'd help her get settled. But I assume we'll be seeing a lot of each other over the next few weeks?"

"Apparently."

"Try to contain your enthusiasm." This time she did smile, quick and slightly mocking and entirely too appealing. "I'll see you around, William."

She walked away before he could respond, rejoining her sister in the crowd, and William stood there with the uncomfortable awareness that he'd just been out-maneuvered by someone with better social skills and a significantly more positive outlook.

The tree lighting countdown began. The crowd pressed closer. Children counted down with the Mayor, ten, nine, eight, and William found himself watching Amy instead of the tree.

She looked up as the lights came on, and her expression transformed. Pure wonder. Pure joy. The kind of reaction that came from someone experiencing something for the first time instead of someone who'd seen it dozens of times and forgotten how to be impressed.

Beside her, Dawn said something that made Amy laugh, that same unguarded laugh he'd noticed earlier, and William felt something shift in his chest that he absolutely did not want to examine.

She was temporary. A consultant passing through. Someone who'd leave the moment the project ended or the town got boring or she remembered she had a real life waiting somewhere else.

Just like Ava.

Except Amy's wonder at the tree lighting hadn't felt performed. And her efficiency hadn't felt like judgment. And the way she'd called him on his skepticism hadn't felt like mockery.

It had felt like someone seeing through his careful distance and deciding to engage anyway.

That was dangerous.

"Beautiful, isn't it?" Mrs. Peterson appeared at his elbow, dabbing her eyes with a handkerchief. "The tree lighting always gets me. And you and that lovely Amy Donovan make such a handsome pair."

"We're not a pair. We're colleagues. Temporarily."

"Of course, dear." She patted his arm with the particular confidence of someone who'd been matchmaking in Holly Falls for forty years and knew better than to believe denials. "Temporarily."

She walked away, and William stood in the crowd watching Amy Donovan laugh with her sister, and tried very hard to convince himself that temporary was exactly what he wanted.

That preserving the past was safer than risking the future.

That noticing someone didn't mean anything except that he had functioning eyes and she was objectively attractive and sometimes the body responded before the brain could shut it down.

He told himself these things with the conviction of someone who'd been telling himself the same lies for three years.

The difference was, this time, he wasn't entirely sure he believed them.

Chapter 3
Amy - December 2nd

The Pleasant Valley Mobile & Electronics store opened at eight o'clock, which Amy knew because she'd been standing outside the door since 7:53, coffee in hand, mentally rehearsing her requirements.

She needed a phone. Not just any phone, she needed her exact model with her exact apps and her exact cloud backup restored so her life could resume its normal, organized trajectory. She'd spent the previous evening on the Evergreen Lodge's complimentary desktop computer, accessing her backups and creating a prioritized list of everything that needed to be re-downloaded, re-synced, and re-organized.

The list had seventeen items.

She'd numbered them by importance.

The door unlocked at exactly 8:00. A teenager with impressive bedhead and a nametag reading "TYLER" looked at her through the glass with the particular resignation of someone who recognized obsessive punctuality when he saw it.

"We just opened," he said as she walked in.

"I know. I need a phone. iPhone 14 Pro, 256GB, silver."

"We might not have that exact... "

"I called yesterday. You have three in stock. I need one, a screen protector, a case, black, not decorative, and someone who can help me

41

restore my cloud backup without asking questions about why I have forty-seven apps."

Tyler blinked. "Okay."

"How long will this take?"

"Depends on your backup size and—"

"How long?"

"Maybe thirty minutes?"

Amy checked her watch. She had breakfast with Dawn at 8:45, which meant she needed to be walking into the Evergreen Lodge dining room in exactly forty-two minutes. Thirty minutes for phone setup left twelve minutes for the walk back, which was cutting it closer than she liked but manageable.

"Let's go."

Twenty-eight minutes later, she had a new phone, a restored backup, and Tyler's slightly shell-shocked expression following her out the door.

Her schedule was intact. Her apps were synced. Her color-coded calendar blocks glowed on the screen like tiny beacons of sanity.

She opened the spreadsheet.

PROJECT: CHRISTMAS HUSBAND stared back at her, all seven tabs present and accounted for.

She should have felt relieved.

Instead, she found herself opening **Tab 3: CANDIDATE DATABASE** and scrolling to entry number four.

4. William Crane, 32, Historian/Business Owner

She'd updated it last night on the lodge computer. The additions sat there in Arial 11-point font, mocking her.

Strengths: Local ties (family business), intelligent (verified: Master's degree), good with hands (verified via observation of shelf repair in background of town hall photo), surprisingly handsome (strong jawline, blue eyes, silver at temples suggests distinguished rather than prematurely aging), owns successful business (antique shop appears well-maintained and profitable based on exterior assessment)

Weaknesses: Excessive cynicism re: holiday traditions (per Dawn: "total Grinch"), resistance to planning, appears commitment-averse based on seven-year gap since last known relationship, irritating know-it-all who lectures about cobblestones, makes assumptions about people based on insufficient data, smug

Compatibility Probability (Preliminary): 63% → REVISED TO 58% based on personality assessment

Status: OBSTACLE - convert to asset?

Notes: Controls access to town archives. Required for Wish Box project. May need to establish a working relationship before pursuing a romantic angle. Strong jawline remains irrelevant but notable. Smells like old books and coffee. Also irrelevant. DELETE THIS NOTE.

She hadn't deleted the note.

Amy closed the spreadsheet and walked toward the Evergreen Lodge, trying not to think about why she'd spent forty-five minutes last night updating William Crane's entry when she should have been reviewing the other sixteen candidates.

Dawn was already at a table when Amy arrived, looking exactly like someone who'd spent the last six months bouncing between European cities with nothing but a backpack and questionable life choices. Her hair was pulled back with what appeared to be a hand-beaded wrap from somewhere exotic. She wore layers, a thermal shirt under a vintage band t-shirt under an oversized cardigan that might have been from the seventies or might have been from last week's thrift store.

She looked happy.

Amy hated how much that observation stung.

"New phone." Dawn nodded at the device Amy set carefully beside her coffee cup. "Let me guess, the exact same model. Already restored from backup. All forty-seven organizational apps reinstalled."

"Only forty-nine, actually. I added two last month."

"Of course you did." Dawn's smile was affectionate rather than mocking, which somehow made it worse. "How's the mission going?"

Amy's coffee cup paused halfway to her mouth. "What mission?"

"The reason you're here. The reason you've been researching Holly Falls demographics like you're planning a military campaign."

"I'm just visiting for Christmas."

"Amy." Dawn leaned forward. "I love you. You're my sister. Which means I know you don't do anything without a plan, a backup plan, and a color-coded spreadsheet tracking your progress."

"That's not... "

"You have a document, don't you? Some kind of organizational system for whatever you're trying to accomplish here."

Amy's fingers tightened on her coffee cup. "Maybe."

"Is it about work? Career stuff?"

"No."

"Then it's about... " Dawn's eyes widened. "Oh my god. You're here to meet someone. You're actually here with a plan to find a boyfriend."

"That's not… I'm not… " Amy stopped. Started again. "Mom keeps asking if I'm bringing someone home for Christmas."

"So?"

"So I'm tired of disappointing her."

"Mom's not disappointed. She's concerned. There's a difference."

"It feels the same from where I'm sitting." Amy pushed eggs around her plate without eating them. "And maybe I'm tired of being the only person at Thanksgiving who eats forty-seven-dollar takeout alone while pretending I'm too busy with work to care."

Dawn's expression softened. "Ames."

"Don't. I'm fine. I'm just being strategic about my social life."

"Strategic."

"Yes."

"You have a spreadsheet of men."

It wasn't a question.

"It's a candidate database," Amy said. "And it's very thorough."

"I don't doubt that." Dawn picked up her coffee, studying Amy over the rim. "How many candidates?"

"That's not important."

"Double digits?"

"Seventeen."

Dawn choked on her coffee. "Seventeen? You made a database of seventeen men?"

"Preliminary research suggests Holly Falls has an above-average ratio of single males in my target demographic. I'm being comprehensive."

"You're being insane."

"I'm being efficient." Amy pulled out her phone, opened the spreadsheet, and turned it so Dawn could see. "Look. I have compatibility probabilities, preliminary assessments, risk mitigation strategies... "

"You have William Crane listed as an obstacle." Dawn's finger hovered over the screen. "With a note about his jawline being irrelevant but notable?"

Amy snatched the phone back. "That's outdated information."

"You updated it last night. There's a timestamp."

"I was being thorough."

"You were being distracted." Dawn's grin was insufferable. "The hot historian got under your skin."

"He's irritating."

"You wrote 'surprisingly handsome.'"

"Objectively handsome. It's a factual observation."

"With a specific note about his jawline."

"I'm deleting that note."

"But you haven't yet." Dawn sat back, looking far too pleased with herself. "This is going to be fun."

"What's going to be fun?"

"Watching you try to organize your way into falling for someone who clearly drives you crazy."

"I'm not falling for anyone. I'm executing a strategic plan to establish a meaningful relationship before Christmas."

"Right. Strategic." Dawn's expression shifted, became gentler. "Amy, you know love doesn't work like that, right? You can't spreadsheet your way to happiness."

"Watch me."

"I have been watching you. For twenty-nine years. And every time you try to control something, it slips through your fingers."

Amy's throat tightened. "That's not fair."

"No, it's not fair, but it's true." Dawn reached across the table and squeezed Amy's hand. "You're allowed to want this. You're allowed to be lonely and scared, and desperate for someone to see you. But making a database of men isn't going to fix what's actually broken."

"Nothing's broken."

"Then why are you here with seventeen names and a color-coded schedule instead of just showing up and seeing what happens?"

Because showing up and seeing what happens was how you ended up alone on Thanksgiving with takeout and regret. Because spontaneity was just another word for failure waiting to happen. Because if she didn't control this, if she didn't plan every step, she might end up with nothing at all.

But she couldn't say any of that.

"I should go," Amy said instead. "I have a meeting with the mayor at nine-thirty."

"About the Wish Box thing?"

"Unfortunately."

"With William?"

"Also, unfortunately."

Dawn's smile returned. "Have fun with your obstacle."

47

"He's not… " Amy stopped. There was no winning this conversation. "I'll see you later."

She left before Dawn could say anything else about jawlines or strategic planning or the particular way Amy's face heated when William Crane's name came up.

Mayor Karen Posey's office looked exactly like someone had asked an interior designer to create a space that screamed "small-town charm" and then given them an unlimited budget and absolutely no supervision. Gingham curtains. A braided rug. Photographs of town events cover every available wall surface. A ceramic cookie jar shaped like a cardinal.

It should have been cozy.

Instead, it felt like being hugged by someone who didn't understand personal space.

Karen sat behind a desk that looked like it was made from reclaimed barn wood, her smile as bright and persistent as the Christmas lights outside. William stood near the window with his arms crossed, seeming like he'd rather be anywhere else.

Amy understood the feeling.

"Thank you both for coming." Karen gestured to the two chairs facing her desk. "Please, sit."

They sat with a single chair-width of space between them, Amy noticed.

She also noticed that he smelled like old books and something woodsy, as if he'd been handling cedar or pine. She told herself that observation was irrelevant.

"I want to be clear about the stakes here," Karen said, folding her hands on the desk with the solemnity of someone about to deliver either very good or very bad news. "The town's community center needs major repairs. The roof is failing. The foundation has structural issues. We're looking at a quarter million dollars in necessary work."

Amy blinked. That was actual money. Real stakes.

"The Christmas Eve gala is our primary fundraiser," Karen continued. "Last year, we raised eighty-two thousand. This year, we need to triple that."

"Triple?" William leaned forward. "Karen, that's not realistic."

"It is if we give people something worth paying for. Something magical. Something that makes them believe." She pulled a folder from her desk drawer. "The Wish Box."

"It's a locked box," William said. "It's been locked for a hundred years."

"Twenty-five years," Karen corrected. "It was last opened in 1999."

Amy's attention sharpened. "It opened?"

"Once. By a couple who'd just moved to town. Margaret and Robert Walters. They were struggling, new business, new marriage, no money, no prospects. They solved the clues, opened the box, and within five years they'd become the town's most successful business owners and its most generous philanthropists."

"Correlation isn't causation," Amy said automatically.

"Maybe not. But it's a good story, and good stories bring donors." Karen opened the folder, revealing what appeared to be a carefully typed document. "The Wish Box legend says it grants the heart's deepest wish to those who prove themselves worthy. The box can only be opened by solving seven clues tied to the town's history."

"Seven clues." Amy was already calculating timelines. Twenty-two days until Christmas Eve. Seven clues meant solving one every three days, give or take. Tight but manageable.

"Each clue leads to the next," Karen said. "The first clue reveals the location of the second, and so on. The final clue supposedly reveals how to open the box itself."

"Supposedly," William repeated. "Because no one knows if that's actually true."

"Margaret and Robert opened it."

"Twenty-five years ago. And they never explained how."

"Which is why you two are going to figure it out," Karen smiled at them with the confident air of someone who'd already decided this would work regardless of anyone else's opinion. "You'll solve the clues, document your process, and present your findings at the gala. The mystery drives ticket sales. The story attracts donors. Everyone wins.

Amy looked at William. He was already watching her, his expression showing he was doing the same mental math she had just finished and coming to the same conclusion: this was going to be a lot more work than either of them expected.

"What if we don't solve all seven clues?" Amy asked.

"Then we present what you've found and spin it as an ongoing mystery. But I believe you'll solve them. You're both very capable people." Karen's smile turned knowing. "And you work well together."

"We don't work together," Amy said. "We had one conversation that ended with both of us trying to escape."

That was working together. You just didn't realize it yet," Karen said as she pulled an envelope from the folder. It was made of cream-colored heavy paper, sealed with actual wax. "This is the first clue."

She broke the seal and unfolded a single sheet of paper. The handwriting was old-fashioned, each letter carefully formed in dark ink.

Karen read aloud:

"Where the first stone was laid, and the first hearth burned bright,
Where founders broke bread in the cold winter night,
Seek the foundation that weathered the years,
The root of our town, now hidden by time.
Beneath ancient timbers and stories now told,
The first of seven secrets waits to unfold."

Silence.

Amy pulled out her phone and started typing notes. Foundation. First hearth. Hidden by years. Ancient timbers.

"You know where it is," she said, glancing at William. He had that look again, the one from yesterday, when he was staring at the Wish Box photograph as if he was seeing something no one else could see.

"The town founder's original cabin," he said. "Built in 1847. It burned down in 1852, but the foundation and part of the original structure were preserved when the new building was constructed on the same site."

"Which building?"

"My shop." He said it without smugness, just stating a fact. "The basement is built around the original cabin's foundation. The old hearthstone is still there."

Of course it was his shop. Naturally, the first clue led straight to the space he managed.

Amy calculated quickly. She needed access to his basement, which meant she had to get him to give it to her. That also meant she had to stay polite, even though he was looking at her like he'd just won something.

What time can we look for it?" she asked.

"We?"

"The clue says 'see,.' and Karen said we're working together, so that is 'we'."

"I can find it myself."

"I'm sure you can. But I'm also sure Karen wants documentation and presentation materials, which means someone needs to take notes, photographs, and create an actual project plan while you're busy communing with your precious cobblestones."

William's jaw clenched. "I don't commune with cobblestones."

"You absolutely commune with cobblestones."

"I document historical artifacts."

"You gently stroke them while reciting their installation dates."

"That happened once... "

"That we know of."

Karen cleared her throat. "Children."

They both looked at her.

'You're working together. That's not optional. William, you provide access and historical context. Amy, you handle organization and documentation. You need each other," her smile sharpens. "Unless you'd like to explain to the town council why the community center is closing because of structural failure."

Cheap shot. Effective, but definitely a low blow.

Amy looked at William. "Ten o'clock. Your shop. Bring a flashlight."

"It's a basement, not a cave."

"Do you have functional lighting in this basement?"

"Define functional."

"Exactly." She stood. "Ten o'clock."

She made it to the door before his voice stopped her.

"Amy."

She turned.

"Bring gloves," he said. "If you're going to handle historical documents, you're doing it properly."

"I know how to handle documents."

"You spilled coffee on a nineteenth-century photograph."

"That was an accident."

"So were most historical disasters. We're preventing yours before it happens."

She wanted to argue, to point out that she was perfectly capable of not destroying priceless artifacts, and to wipe that insufferable knowing expression off his stupidly handsome face.

Instead, she said, "Fine. Gloves. Anything else, Professor?"

"Don't be late."

"I'm never late."

"We'll see."

She walked out before she said something that would definitely end up in his mental notes file under "reasons Amy Donovan is impossible to work with."

The town square was busy at mid-morning, with people moving between shops and voices echoing in the cold air. Amy pulled out her phone to check her schedule; she had forty-seven minutes before meeting William, which was enough time to get better coffee than the lodge offered and maybe review her notes on the first clue.

Then she heard laughter, children's laughter, high and delighted.

She looked up.

A child was running across the square, full-speed, arms pumping, dark curls bouncing. Maybe three years old. Wearing a pink coat with the hood flying behind her like a cape. No adult in immediate pursuit.

Dawn appeared from the coffee shop entrance, saw the child, and moved.

Not frantically. Not panicked. Just quickly, intercepting the child's trajectory with the ease of someone who'd done this before. She crouched, caught the toddler mid-run, and lifted her up, spinning her around.

The child shrieked with delight.

"Going somewhere, speed demon?" Dawn's voice carried across the square, warm and laughing.

"Flying!"

"I can see that. You're very fast."

"Lily!" A man jogged up, slightly breathless. Tall, broad-shouldered, wearing work clothes and an expression of mingled relief and exhaustion. "I turned around for two seconds... "

"She's quick." Dawn set her down but kept hold of her hand. "Like a tiny, extremely determined rocket."

"I'm so sorry. She's usually not... " He stopped, actually seeing Dawn for the first time. His expression shifted. "Hi."

"Hi." Dawn's smile gentled. "You must be her dad."

"Jack. Jack Forester. And this is Lily." He rested a hand on his daughter's curly head. "Who is apparently training for the Olympic sprinting team without telling me."

She has good form. She's a natural athlete.

"Natural escape artist." But he was smiling now, the exhaustion easing. "Thank you for catching her."

"Anytime. I'm Dawn." She crouched to Lily's level. "You've got to give your dad a break, speed demon. He's working hard to keep up with you."

"You're pretty." Lily touched Dawn's beaded hair wrap. "Sparkly."

"Thank you. You're pretty too, and incredibly fast."

Jack was still staring at Dawn. Not in a creepy way, but like people look at surprising things that make them happy.

Amy recognized that look. She had catalogued it seventeen times in her research. That was interest. Real interest. The kind that bypassed logic and planning and sensible assessment.

The kind she'd never managed to inspire.

Dawn stood and handed Lily's hand to Jack. Their fingers brushed. Both of them noticed. Neither moved away immediately.

"I should let you go," Dawn said.

"Yeah. Yeah, we should go... " Jack looked down at his daughter. "Say thank you, Lily."

"Thank you for catching me."

"You're welcome. Maybe next time, give your dad a warning before you take off?"

"Okay." Lily paused. "You smell like flowers."

Dawn laughed. "Jasmine. It's my favorite."

"I like it." Lily tugged her father's hand. "Can we get a snack now?"

"Sure, sweetheart." But Jack was still looking at Dawn. "Do you, are you staying in town for a while?"

"Through New Year."

"That's good. That's... maybe I'll see you around?"

"Maybe." Dawn's smile held something Amy couldn't quite name. Not her usual easy warmth. Something softer. More careful. "Take care of your speed demon."

"I'll try." Jack let Lily pull him toward the bakery, but he looked back twice.

Dawn watched them go, her expression unreadable.

Amy walked over. "New friend?"

Dawn jumped. "Amy. I didn't see you."

"I noticed. You were busy catching runaway children."

"She's fast. And adorable." Dawn was still watching the bakery entrance where Jack and Lily had disappeared. "Did you see her curls? They're perfect."

"I saw you holding her father's hand longer than necessary."

"I was returning his daughter. That's called being helpful."

"That's called being interested."

"I'm not... " Dawn stopped. Laughed. "Okay, fine. He's cute. And clearly devoted to his kid. There's something appealing about a man who sprints after a child without complaining."

"You're staying here for four weeks."

"So?"

"So you don't do four weeks. You do cities and countries and moving on before anyone can ask you to stay."

Dawn's expression shifted. "Maybe I'm tired of moving."

"Are you?"

"I don't know." She looked at the bakery again. "But something about the town feels different. Like maybe it's worth staying for."

Amy thought about William, his cobblestones, and his basement full of history. About how he'd looked at the Christmas tree as if it truly mattered. About the spreadsheet entry she kept updating with irrelevant details about jawlines and book smells.

"Yeah," she said quietly. "Maybe it is."

They stood there together, two sisters who had spent their lives fleeing different things, observing a small town go about its morning routines.

Amy checked her watch.

Twenty-nine minutes until she had to meet William.

Twenty-nine minutes to review her notes, organize her approach, and prepare for an afternoon in a basement with a man who made her want to rewrite all her carefully crafted plans.

She opened her phone. Looked at the spreadsheet.

Status: OBSTACLE, convert to asset?

Her finger hovered over the edit button.

Then she closed the app and walked toward William's shop, trying very hard not to estimate the chance that this was going to end badly.

The number kept appearing anyway.

Approximately 73%.

She went anyway.

Chapter 4
William - December 4th

William had expected Amy to be early. He had not expected her to arrive with a leather messenger bag containing what appeared to be an entire office supply store.

She stood in his shop at exactly 9:58, two minutes before their scheduled meeting, wearing dark jeans and a cream sweater under a quilted vest. Her hair was pulled back in a ponytail that looked practical rather than fashionable. She had brought a notebook, the expensive kind with an elastic closure, along with a digital camera, a small tablet, and what appeared to be color-coded sticky notes.

"You came prepared," he said.

"I believe in documentation." She looked around the shop with the focused attention of someone conducting an assessment. "Your online presence doesn't do this place justice."

"My online presence?"

"Your website. It's functional but minimal. No virtual tour, limited inventory photos, and operating hours that haven't been updated since 2019." She pulled out her tablet and showed him his own website, as if he hadn't seen it. "You could be generating significantly more traffic with better SEO optimization and a more robust social media strategy."

"I like my current traffic levels."

"You like having an empty shop on weekday mornings?"

"I like having time to preserve the items people bring me instead of performing for tourists with cameras."

She made a note on her tablet. Actually made a note, as if she were cataloging his deficiencies for future reference.

"What are you writing?" he asked.

"Observations. You're resistant to modernization, which tracks with your general personality profile."

"I don't have a personality profile."

Everyone has a personality profile. Yours indicates someone who values tradition more than progress, prefers solitude over socializing, and finds comfort in objects rather than in people.

She wasn't wrong. That was the annoying part.

"Are you analyzing me or helping me find a clue?"

"I can do both. I'm very efficient." She closed the tablet, returned it to her bag with the particular care of someone who'd organized every pocket by category. "So. The basement."

"The archives," he corrected. "It's not just a basement."

"Right. The archives." She said it like someone humoring a child. "Where you keep the historically significant foundation of a cabin that burned down in 1852."

"The foundation is structurally integrated into the building. We're not going into a separate space; we're accessing the original construction that everything else was built around."

"So it's a basement with old rocks."

"It's a preserved archaeological site with cultural significance."

"You really take this seriously."

"Someone should." He walked toward the back of the shop, where a door marked PRIVATE led to the stairs. "The lighting isn't great. The ceiling is low in places. And it's December, so it's going to be cold."

"I brought a flashlight." She pulled a small LED light from her bag, because of course she had.

"Of course you did." He unlocked the door and flipped the switch that controlled the basement lights. A series of bare bulbs flickered to life, casting uneven illumination down a steep, narrow staircase. "Watch your step. The treads are original, built in 1852 when they were reconstructed after the fire."

"You mean they're uneven and can be dangerous."

"I mean, they're historical."

"Those aren't mutually exclusive." But she followed him down, her flashlight beam bouncing off the stone walls.

The temperature dropped with each step. The air smelled like old wood and damp earth and dust, the particular scent of spaces that had been sealed away from the world for decades. The stairs were steep enough that William had to duck his head at the bottom, where the ceiling beam crossed low.

Amy's flashlight swept across the space, and he heard her breath catch.

The basement wasn't large, maybe twenty feet by thirty, with a ceiling that averaged seven feet high but dropped to six in the corners where the original foundation met the newer construction. The walls were a mix of old stone and newer brick, with the transitions visible in the mortar work. At the far end, the original hearthstone rose from the floor, a massive granite slab that had somehow survived the fire that destroyed everything around it.

Shelves lined the walls, packed with boxes of town records, property deeds, photographs, and minutes from historical society meetings going back to 1889. A work table sat in the center, covered with documents William had been cataloging before the Wish Box project had derailed his entire schedule.

"This is…" Amy's voice sounded smaller than usual. Tighter. "This is a lot of history."

"Seventy-three boxes of town records. Forty-two years of meeting minutes. Three hundred and sixteen photographs, some dating back to the 1880s." He moved toward the work table and turned on the desk lamp. "Everything that matters about this town's past is in this room."

"Everything that fits in a basement, anyway."

"Everything that's been preserved." He looked at her, found her standing very close to the stairs, her flashlight gripped tightly. "You okay?"

"Fine."

"You don't look fine."

"I'm fine. I don't care for enclosed spaces." She took a breath and visibly steadied herself. "Especially underground enclosed spaces with questionable ceiling stability."

The ceiling is completely stable. This building successfully passed the structural inspection last year.

That's very reassuring," but she still hadn't moved away from the stairs.

William recognized avoidance when he saw it. He'd spent enough time around his own fears to know what they looked like on someone else's face.

"My grandfather built this place," he said, keeping his voice casual, giving her something to focus on beyond the walls pressing in. "Not the original cabin, obviously. But when he bought the property in 1967, the foundation was still there, just buried under decades of neglect. He excavated it, preserved it, and built the shop around it specifically so this space would stay intact.

"Why?" She took a step forward, closer to the table, farther from the stairs. Progress.

"Because he believed that history matters, that the stories we tell about where we came from shape who we become. This foundation—" He rested his hand on the nearest stone wall. "This is where Holly Falls started. Four families, one cabin, the middle of winter in 1847. They shouldn't have survived. But they did, because they preserved what mattered and built something new around it."

Amy moved closer, her attention shifting from the ceiling to the walls, then to the hearthstone at the far end. "That's why you do this. The antique shop, the historical society, all of it. You're trying to be like your grandfather."

"I'm trying to finish what he started. He died before he could complete the cataloging project. Left me boxes of unsorted documents and a note that said, 'Make sure they remember.'"

"Remember what?"

"Everything. Every small moment, every ordinary day. The big events are automatically remembered: wars, disasters, and celebrations. But the small things, the daily life, that's what gets lost. And that's what tells you who people were."

She was beside him now, looking at the boxes with a different expression. Not an assessment anymore. Something closer to understanding.

I didn't choose consulting; I simply fell into it. It was measurable, clear, logical, with no room for chance. When everything else felt chaotic, I needed that certainty. After my parents' divorce, after my dad got sick, and after everything seemed to be falling apart, I needed to prove I could fix broken systems and make them work, that I could create order from chaos.

He looked at her. She was still holding the flashlight, but her grip had loosened. Her shoulders had dropped from their defensive position.

"Did it work?" he asked.

"For everything except my personal life." A brief smile, self-deprecating. "Turns out you can't spreadsheet your way to happiness. Who knew?"

"But you're still trying."

"I don't know what else to do." She looked at him directly, and her eyes were that shifting hazel again, more green than brown in the uneven light. "This town, this whole situation with the Wish Box, I didn't plan for any of this. And I don't know how to function when I'm not following a plan."

"You could try improvising."

"That's just a fancy word for flailing."

"Or it's a fancy word for being alive."

They stood there, too close together in the small space, and William felt a change between them. Not attraction, though that was there. More like recognition. Two people who'd spent years building walls suddenly saw that their foundations were nearly the same.

"The hearthstone," Amy said, breaking the moment. "That's where the clue would be hidden, right? 'Where the first stone was laid and the first hearth burned bright.'"

"Probably." He moved toward it, grateful for the task, for something to do besides stand there, noticing the way she'd said "improvising" as if it were a foreign language she was trying to learn. "My grandfather found the original cornerstone when he excavated. It had markings carved into it, names, dates, coordinates."

The hearthstone was massive, easily six feet long and three feet wide, raised about eight inches from the floor. Time and heat had darkened the granite to nearly black, but the surface was smooth, polished by decades of use.

Amy crouched beside it, running her flashlight beam across the surface. "I don't see anything."

"It wouldn't be visible from this angle. The markings are underneath, where it meets the foundation." He knelt beside her, close quarters now, their shoulders nearly touching. "We'll need to look at the base."

She leaned forward, directing her flashlight beam into the narrow gap between the stone and the floor. "There's something carved here. Can you see it?"

He shifted closer, his head near hers, both of them bent over the same small space. He could smell her shampoo, something clean and citrus-forward, practical rather than floral.

"There." She pointed, and her hand brushed his shoulder as she reached. She pulled back with a small jerk. "Sorry."

"It's fine. Tight space." But he still was aware of where she'd touched him, which was ridiculous.

He focused on the carving instead. Old chisel marks, weathered but still visible. Letters formed in the archaic style of the mid-1800s.

Amy pulled out her camera, took several photos from different angles. Then she retrieved her notebook and started sketching what they could see, her hand moving quickly across the page.

"You draw," he said.

"I document. There's a difference."

"Your sketch is very good."

"Thank you. I took technical drawing in college. It's useful for creating accurate records." She finished the sketch, labeled it with the date and location. "What does it say?"

He leaned closer, traced the letters with his finger. "'*Beneath this stone, the heart begins. Where water first blessed this ground, seek the center of all things.*'"

"The heart that beats beneath the town," Amy murmured. "Water source. The original well?"

"There's a decorative fountain in the town square now, but it's built over the original well from 1847. That's where the second clue would be."

"So we've solved the first clue." She sat back, looked pleased with herself. "That was faster than I expected."

"You expected it to take longer?"

"I expected more arguing about procedure."

"We could argue if you want. I noticed you started with documentation before examining the historical context."

"And I noticed you went for narrative significance instead of photographic evidence. But we got to the same answer, so maybe our methods are complementary."

"Complementary." He tested the word. "That's one way to put it."

"What would you call it?"

"Surprisingly effective." He stood and offered her a hand up.

She looked at his hand for a moment before taking it. Her fingers were cold from the basement air, and when he pulled her up, she stumbled a little on the uneven floor.

His other hand shot out in an instant, steadying her by the elbow.

They were very close now. Close enough that he could see the way her pupils had dilated in the dim light. Close enough to notice the small scar on her chin that he'd missed before.

"Thanks," she said, not moving away.

"The floor is a little uneven."

"Right. The historically significant, potentially dangerous floor."

"It's not dangerous if you watch where you're stepping."

"I was watching. I was also thinking about the clue."

"Multitasking in a basement. Bold choice."

She laughed, a short, surprised sound, then stepped back, establishing proper distance between them. "We should document the rest of this space. Take measurements, photographs, and create a record of what we found."

"You want to catalog my basement?"

"I want to catalog the historically significant archaeological site that happens to be in your basement, yes."

"That'll take at least an hour."

"Then it's good I brought extra batteries for my camera." She was already moving toward the hearthstone, the camera in her hands, the earlier nervousness about enclosed spaces forgotten now that she had a project to focus on.

William watched her work, the methodical way she photographed each section, the neat labels she created in her notebook, the systematic approach that should have been tedious but somehow wasn't.

She was good at this. Not just competent, but good. She understood the difference between documenting for the sake of completion and documenting to preserve meaning.

"Why consulting?" he asked after she'd finished photographing the hearthstone from eight different angles. "If you're this good at research and documentation, why not history or archiving?"

She looked up from her notebook. "Consulting pays better."

"That's not a real answer."

"No, but it's a practical answer."

"Practical isn't the same as honest."

She set down the camera and leaned against the work table. The defensive walls were coming back up; he could see it happening in real time.

"I needed something with clear metrics," she said finally. "In consulting, you have deliverables. Deadlines. Success criteria. You know if you're doing well or failing. There's no ambiguity."

"And history is ambiguous."

"History is interpretation. You can spend your whole life researching something and still not know if you got it right. I don't do well with uncertainty."

"So you chose a career where you could control the outcome."

"I chose a career where I could be useful. Where I could prove my worth in measurable ways." She straightened and picked up the camera again. "Can we look at the documents on the table? You said you'd been cataloging town records."

He let her change the subject partly because he recognized the need to retreat when vulnerability became uncomfortable, mostly because he was starting to understand that Amy Donovan's walls were built from the same material as his, fear disguised as practicality.

They spent the next forty minutes going through boxes, with Amy photographing key documents while William provided context. They developed a rhythm; she'd pull a document, he'd explain its significance, she'd photograph and catalog it, and they'd move to the next.

They reached for the same deed at one point, their hands colliding.

"Sorry," she said.

"My fault." But neither of them pulled back yet.

The deed was old, the paper fragile, the handwriting elaborate. William could feel the warmth of her hand beside his, could see the way her fingers hesitated before withdrawing.

She cleared her throat. "What is it?"

"The original land grant from 1847. This is what established Holly Falls as an official settlement."

"That's significant."

"Very."

"You should have special preservation conditions for this."

"I do. Temperature-controlled storage, acid-free folders, limited light exposure."

"You really care about this stuff."

"It's my job to care."

"No." She looked at him directly. "It's more than that. You love it. The stories, the objects, the way they connect to people you'll never meet. You love getting to be the one who preserves what they left behind."

He never expressed it that way. He never allowed himself to admit that it was love instead of duty. But she was right.

"Yeah," he said quietly. "I do."

They finished the cataloging. Amy packed up her equipment with the same systematic care she'd used to unpack it. William watched her organize her bag, every item returned to its designated pocket, and wondered when organizational neuroses had started seeming endearing rather than exhausting.

"Coffee?" he asked as they climbed back up the stairs into the shop. "There's a place two doors down. They make decent lattes."

She pulled out her phone, opened what was clearly a calendar app, and stared at the screen for a long moment.

"I don't have anything scheduled right now," she said, like she was confessing something shameful. "I blocked this time for the basement search, but I built in three extra hours as a buffer for potential complications, and we finished early, so technically I'm free until two-thirty when I have... nothing. I have nothing at two-thirty."

"Did you just realize you've been scheduling fake appointments?"

"I've been building in contingency time. That's different."

"Is it?"

She closed the phone. "Coffee sounds good."

The Bean Counter was what it sounded like, a coffee shop run by an accountant who'd gotten tired of accounting. The owner, Michael Watson, waved when they entered.

"William. Amy." He said their names together, like they were a unit. "The usual?"

"You don't know my usual," Amy pointed out. "I've never been here."

"Black coffee, no sugar, because you think ordering anything fancier makes you high maintenance?" Michael grinned at her surprise. "Dawn talks about you. A lot. She's worried."

"Dawn worries too much."

"Dawn is a smart woman who knows her sister." He turned to William. "Americano?"

"Please."

"Coming up. Grab a seat. I'll bring them over."

They found a table near the window. The shop was quiet, a mid-morning lull between breakfast rush and lunch crowd. Two other tables occupied, both by people William recognized, but who thankfully seemed content to leave them alone.

"He's on your list," William said.

Amy looked up sharply. "What?"

"Michael. He's one of your seventeen candidates."

"I don't know what you're talking about."

"Dawn mentioned you made a database of eligible bachelors. Michael Watson, accountant-turned-coffee-shop-owner, age thirty-two, financially stable, local ties. He fits your criteria."

Her face went through several expressions in rapid succession: denial, embarrassment, defiance, before settling on resignation. "Fine. Yes. He's on the list. Number one, actually."

"And?"

"And what?"

"Are you interested?"

She looked at Michael, who was currently making their drinks with focused attention. "He seems nice. Attractive. Stable."

"That's not what I asked."

"What do you want me to say? That I have some instant chemistry with him? That I took one look and knew he was my soulmate?" She wrapped her hands around the water glass Michael had brought. "I don't believe in that. I believe in compatibility metrics and shared values and building something functional over time."

"That sounds romantic."

"It sounds realistic. Romance is just brain chemistry wearing a fancy hat. The hat falls off eventually, and what you're left with is whether two people can build a life together."

"You've given this a lot of thought."

"I give everything a lot of thought. It's my defining characteristic." She met his eyes. "What about you? You clearly don't believe in databases and compatibility algorithms. So what do you believe in?"

"I believe in paying attention. In noticing the small things, the way someone looks at a Christmas tree, or how they organize their bag, or whether they're brave enough to go into a basement that scares them because they said they would."

"That's very observational."

"I'm a historian. Observation is the job."

"And what have you observed about me?"

Her fear of being alone was clear. She masked her vulnerability with efficiency because it felt too risky. She observed everything but acted as if she didn't notice. She smelled like citrus, arranged her life in color-coded sections, and bore a scar on her chin from a childhood mishap, which was recorded in a spreadsheet somewhere.

That she was the most interesting person he'd met in three years, and he had no idea how to handle that information.

"I've observed that you're very thorough," he said instead.

"That's a diplomatic answer."

"I'm being diplomatic."

"Why?"

"Because the honest answer would be inappropriate for a professional working relationship."

Her eyes widened. Her cheeks flushed. "Oh."

Michael arrived with their coffee, breaking the moment. "One black coffee, boring and efficient. One Americano for the man who thinks espresso is a personality trait."

"Thank you, Michael," William said.

"Anytime. Amy, if you need anything else, and I mean anything, you just let me know. We take care of Dawn's family around here."

He left before Amy could respond.

She stared at her coffee. "He's very nice."

"He is."

"Number one on the list. Stable. Attractive. Kind."

"All excellent qualities."

"So why does this feel weird?"

"What feels weird?"

"Sitting here with you, drinking coffee, talking about my database of eligible bachelors like it's a normal thing instead of evidence that I need therapy."

William smiled despite himself. "Maybe because you're realizing that the list isn't helping."

"The list is a tool. Tools are helpful by definition."

"Unless you're using a hammer to paint a picture."

She laughed, that short, surprised sound he was starting to recognize. "Are you calling my list a hammer?"

"I'm suggesting that maybe you're using the wrong tool for the job."

"And what's the right tool?"

He looked at her across the table, at the way the sunlight caught in her hair, at the small smile playing at the corner of her mouth.

"I don't know," he said honestly. "But I think it involves less planning and more paying attention to what's happening instead of what you think should happen."

"That's terrifying advice."

"Probably."

"You're enjoying this. Watching me struggle with uncertainty."

"I'm enjoying watching you be honest about struggling with uncertainty. There's a difference."

Before she could respond, a voice interrupted.

"Well, isn't this lovely?" Mrs. Peterson appeared beside their table, wearing a purple coat and a smile that suggested she'd just witnessed something significant. "William Crane and Amy Donovan, having coffee together like a proper couple."

"We're not—" Amy started.

"We're working on the Wish Box project," William said.

"Of course you are, dear. That's what I said to Martha, almost word for word, this morning. I said, 'Martha, those two are going to make a lovely pair.' And look at you, proving me right."

"Mrs. Peterson," William said carefully, "we're colleagues."

"For now." She patted his shoulder. "Have a good day, you two. Don't work too hard."

She bustled away, leaving silence in her wake.

"This town is very invested in other people's business," Amy said.

"It's a small town. Other people's business is the primary entertainment."

"That's horrifying."

"That's community."

"Same thing." She checked her phone, though William suspected it was more habit than necessity. "I should go. I need to... I should have something I need to do."

"But you don't."

"I should generate something. It's unsettling not having a schedule."

"You could let yourself be unsettled."

"Or I could create a detailed plan for investigating the town fountain tomorrow."

"We could do both."

She looked at him. "Are you suggesting we meet again tomorrow?"

"The second clue is at the fountain. We should investigate together. For efficiency's sake."

"Right. Efficiency." She was giving a slight grin. "What time?"

"Ten?"

"I'll be there." She stood and gathered her bag. "Thank you. For the basement tour. And the coffee."

"Thank you for not destroying any more irreplaceable historical documents."

"The day's not over yet."

He watched her leave, saw the way she moved around tables with that same purposeful stride, observed her pause at the door and glance back at him for just a moment before stepping out into the December cold.

Michael appeared beside him. "So I'm number one on the list, huh?"

"You heard that?"

I hear everything. It's a curse," Michael said as he collected their empty cups. "But for what it's worth, I think you're higher on her list than she's admitting."

"She just met me."

"Sometimes that's all it takes." Michael grinned. "See you tomorrow, Will. Try not to fall for the woman with the spreadsheet."

"I'm not falling for anyone."

"Sure you're not."

William sat there after Michael left, watching the town square through the window, observing people go about their day, and he tried very hard not to think about hazel eyes that changed color and how Amy had grabbed his arm in the basement when the walls felt like they were closing in.

He failed.

Tomorrow, they'll investigate the fountain to find the second clue. Continue this professional collaboration that was definitely not turning into something more.

He almost believed it.

Chapter 5

Amy - December 5th

The fountain in the town square was installed in 1952, as indicated by the brass plaque on its base. It is now more decorative than functional, shut off for the winter, with its basin empty except for a few dead leaves and what appeared to be a decades-old penny someone had tossed in for luck.

Amy slowly circled it, camera in hand, taking photos of the stonework from all angles while William examined the inscription that went around the rim.

"It's Latin," he said, running his fingers along the carved letters. "I can make out a few words, but not enough for a complete translation."

"You don't read Latin?" Amy lowered her camera, surprised. "I thought historians were required to read old languages."

"I can stumble through basic translations with a dictionary and enough time, but this—" He gestured at the ornate script. "This is beyond my ability. We need someone fluent."

"Do you know anyone fluent in Latin in Holly Falls?"

"Father Matthews. He's retired now, but he taught at the Catholic school for forty years. If anyone can translate this, he can."

Amy pulled out her phone, opened her notes app. "Do you have his number?"

"I'll call him." William pulled out his own phone, an older model, probably three generations behind, no case, screen cracked on one side. He noticed her noticing. "It works."

"I didn't say anything."

"You were thinking it."

"I was thinking you should invest in a screen protector."

"I should invest in many things. A new phone screen isn't high on the list." He dialed, waited. "Father Matthews? It's William Crane. I'm sorry to bother you, but I need a Latin inscription translated... Yes, for the Wish Box project... At the fountain in the square... You can? That's... thank you. We'll be here."

He hung up. "He'll be here in twenty minutes. He's excited. Translating mysterious Latin inscriptions is more interesting than his usual Thursday morning, I guess."

"What does he usually do on Thursday mornings?"

"Crossword puzzles and complaining about how the New York Times has gotten too easy."

Twenty minutes. Amy checked her phone calendar out of habit, saw the empty block of time she'd labeled "Fountain Investigation - BUFFER: 2 hrs" and felt that familiar discomfort that came with unstructured waiting.

"We could review our notes while we wait," she suggested. "Cross-reference what we've found so far, create a timeline of clue progression—"

"Or we could sit." William settled onto the stone edge of the fountain and pulled a thermos from his backpack pocket. "I brought hot chocolate. Want some?"

She stared at the thermos. "You brought hot chocolate to a clue investigation."

"I brought hot chocolate to a December morning in Vermont. The clue investigation is incidental." He unscrewed the cap and poured steaming liquid into it. The smell of chocolate and something spiced, cinnamon, maybe cardamom, drifted toward her. "It's from the bakery. They make it properly. None of that instant packet nonsense."

"I wasn't going to criticize your hot chocolate sourcing."

"You were thinking it."

"I was thinking you're very prepared for someone who says they prefer spontaneity over planning."

"There's a difference between planning for comfort and planning for control." He held out the cup. "This is the former."

She took it. Sat beside him on the cold stone, leaving a respectable distance between them. The hot chocolate was exactly as advertised, rich, spiced as it should be, the kind that required actual chocolate rather than powder.

"This is really good," she admitted.

"Told you." He poured himself a cup from the thermos and cradled it in both hands. "The bakery owner is Jack's sister. She's been perfecting this recipe for fifteen years."

"Jack. The guy with the daughter."

"The one Dawn seems interested in, yes."

Amy sipped her hot chocolate and watched people cross the square, going about their ordinary Thursday business. A woman walking a dog. Two teenagers arguing about something with the passionate intensity only teenagers could muster. An elderly man is feeding pigeons despite the sign that specifically requests people not to feed the pigeons.

"This is nice," she said, then immediately regretted it because "nice" sounded insipid, and she sounded like someone who didn't know how to sit quietly with another person without filling the silence with productivity.

"It is." William didn't seem to find her observation insipid. "You don't do this much, do you? Just sit."

"I sit. I sit all the time. I sit at my desk, I sit in meetings, I sit on the subway—"

"That's not what I mean."

She knew what he meant. "No. I don't do this much."

"Why not?"

"Because sitting without purpose feels like wasting time. And wasting time feels like failing."

"At what?"

"At everything." She wrapped both hands around the cup, letting the warmth seep into her fingers. "At being productive, being useful, being worth the space I take up in the world."

He was quiet for a moment. When he spoke, his voice was careful. "That's a lot of pressure to put on yourself."

"It's realistic. The world doesn't owe me anything just for existing. I have to earn my place in it."

"By never stopping?"

"By never failing."

"Those aren't the same thing."

"They feel the same."

He shifted to one side, not quite turning toward her but angling his body in her direction. "What happens if you fail?"

"I don't know. I've spent my entire adult life making sure I don't find out."

She pulled her phone out of her pocket, saw zero notifications, and felt a small spike of anxiety that nothing was requiring her immediate attention.

William noticed. Of course he noticed. "Expecting something important?"

"No. Just checking."

"For what?"

"For anything. For proof that I'm needed somewhere by someone for something." She put the phone away, felt foolish. "That sounds pathetic."

"It sounds human."

"Same thing."

They sat in silence, not comfortable exactly, but not entirely uncomfortable either—more like two people learning how to exist in the same space without performing for each other.

Amy found herself noticing things. The way William's hair curled at the nape of his neck. The small scar on his knuckles she'd seen before but not really looked at. The way he held his cup with both hands, as if he needed the warmth.

"Father Matthews is here," William said, nodding toward an elderly man approaching with the energetic stride of someone decades younger.

The priest was maybe seventy, with white hair and keen eyes under bushy brows. He wore a heavy coat over what appeared to be a cardigan and dress pants, and he carried a well-used leather notebook.

"William, my boy." Father Matthews patted William on the shoulder. "And you must be Amy. Dawn's sister. I've heard great things."

"From Dawn?"

"From everyone. Small town." He pulled reading glasses from his pocket and settled them on his nose. "Now, show me this mysterious Latin."

They showed him the inscription. He bent close, tracing the letters with one finger, murmuring to himself in what Amy assumed was Latin.

"Fascinating," he said after a moment. "This is quite old. The phrasing suggests late medieval construction, though the fountain itself is obviously modern."

"Can you translate it?" William asked.

"Of course. It says: 'Ubi risus puerorum per hiemem resonat, ibi cor oppidi vivit.' Which translates roughly to: 'Where children's laughter echoes through winter, there the heart of the town lives.'"

Amy was already pulling out her notebook. "Children's laughter. Winter. Heart of the town."

"The community center," William said. "The Nativity play rehearsals start this week. Every winter, dozens of kids, constant laughter, and chaos."

"The heart of the town," Father Matthews agreed. "The community center has been the gathering place for Holly Falls families since it was built in 1963. If you're looking for where children's laughter echoes through winter, that's your answer."

"Thank you, Father." William shook his hand. "This helps enormously."

"My pleasure. I haven't had this much fun with Latin since that graduate student tried to get me to translate his tattoo after he got it inked." Father Matthews's eyes twinkled. "Turns out 'strength and honor' is much harder to translate accurately than one might think. He ended up with something closer to 'poison of little man.'"

Amy laughed before she could stop herself. "He didn't."

"He absolutely did. Wore long sleeves for six months until he could afford the removal." Father Matthews tucked his notebook back into his pocket. "Good luck with your quest, you two. And Amy? Don't let this one's grumpy historian act fool you. He's softer than he pretends."

He walked away before either of them could respond.

"Softer than you pretend," Amy repeated. "That's quite an endorsement."

"Father Matthews has known me since I was eight. He's biased."

"Or he's observant."

"Same thing."

They walked toward the community center, following the sounds of chaos before they even reached the door. Children's voices, high and excited. Adult voices, trying unsuccessfully to wrangle the excitement into something resembling order.

William opened the door, and they stepped into controlled pandemonium.

The community center's main room had been transformed into a space that felt like a cross between a rehearsal area and a costume explosion. A makeshift stage sat at one end, complete with a wooden stable that looked kind of shaky. Children ranged in age from about four to twelve, some wearing bathrobes that were standing in for biblical robes, while others dressed normally with construction paper halos taped to their heads.

Amy stood in the doorway, overwhelmed by the sheer volume of noise and motion.

William stepped into it as if he belonged there.

"Hey, Tommy." He caught a running child, maybe six years old, wearing a bathrobe and carrying a stuffed sheep. "Where's the fire?"

"I'm not Tommy, I'm a shepherd." The child was deeply offended. "Shepherds have sheep."

"My apologies. Where's the shepherd fire?"

"There's no fire. We're following the star." He pointed at a cardboard star someone had hung from the ceiling.

"Excellent following. Carry on."

The child ran off, sheep clutched to his chest.

A little girl approached next, maybe seven, wearing a crooked tinfoil crown. "Are you married?"

Amy froze. "What?"

"You and him." The girl pointed at William. "Are you married?"

"No," Amy said quickly. "We're just... we're working together."

"On what?"

"A project. A historical project about the town."

"That sounds boring."

"It's quite interesting, to tell the truth."

"You look at each other nice," the girl said with the blunt observation only children could manage. "Like my mom and dad look at each other. You should be married."

Amy's face burned. "That's not—we're not—"

William's ears had gone red. "We should find the clue."

"Definitely. The clue. Where would it be?" Amy looked around desperately for anything that might distract from the fact that a seven-year-old had just identified something Amy had been trying very hard not to acknowledge.

"The manger." William pointed toward the stage. "The original town Nativity used an actual manger that dated back to the 1890s. If there's a clue here, I think that's where it would be."

They approached the stage. The manger was clearly a prop, painted wood, filled with straw that looked suspiciously like the kind you bought at craft stores. But underneath the straw, Amy could see older wood. Weathered, worn, genuine.

William moved the straw to the side, revealing carved text on the inside of the manger's back panel.

Amy photographed it while William read aloud: "'Where vows were first spoken and promises made, seek the foundation of faith that won't fade.'"

"The chapel," Amy said. "The historic chapel where the town's first wedding was held."

"That's the one." William was already making notes in his own small notebook, handwritten, no digital backup, the kind of record-keeping that would make Amy's organizational soul weep. "We'll need to get the key. It's kept locked except for special events."

"Do you have access?"

"I can get access."

"William!" A woman's voice called out. Amy turned to see a woman in her thirties approaching, clipboard in hand, looking harassed. "Thank God. Can you help me with the angel choir? They're supposed to be practicing their song, but three of them are fighting over who gets to wear the biggest wings."

"I can try." William looked at Amy. "Give me five minutes?"

"Take your time. I'll document the manger." And try to stop thinking about children who had better romantic intuition than she did.

He disappeared into the chaos, and Amy watched him crouch beside a group of children in white sheets with cardboard wings taped to their backs. He said something that made them laugh. Within thirty seconds, they were lined up, wings adjusted, ready to sing.

He was good with kids. Natural around them. Patient in a way that showed genuine affection rather than obligation.

Amy added that to her mental file of "Things About William Crane That Are Irrelevant But Notable" and tried not to think about what it meant that the file was getting longer every day.

"He's good with them."

Amy turned. Dawn stood beside her, holding a pile of fabric that looked like more costume pieces. Lily was tucked against her side, one small hand fisted in Dawn's sweater.

"He seems comfortable," Amy agreed.

Jack says William's the first person kids turn to when they're upset about town events. Something about him makes them feel safe. Dawn shifted, and Lily shifted with her. Smiling down at her, she said, "Right, speed demon? Safe people are good people."

Lily nodded solemnly, then buried her face in Dawn's sweater.

Amy watched her sister with this child who wasn't hers, watched the easy way Dawn comforted her, the easy way Lily settled against her.

"You're good with her," Amy said.

"She's easy to be good with." Dawn's voice was soft. "Sweet kid. Brave kid. Lost her mom when she was a baby, but Jack's doing an incredible job raising her."

"You're thinking about staying, aren't you? Not just through New Year. Longer."

Dawn met her eyes. "Maybe. I don't know. It's terrifying."

"Because staying means you might have to build something real instead of just visiting other people's real things."

"Says the woman with seventeen men on a spreadsheet."

"Touché." Amy looked back at William, who was now helping a child adjust a shepherd's hook. "How do you know when it's worth the risk? Staying, building, committing to something that might not work out?"

"You don't know. That's the whole point. You just decide the possibility is worth more than the safety."

Before Amy could respond, Jack appeared, slightly breathless. "There you are. Lily, sweetheart, we have to go. Grandma's waiting for us at home."

"Don't want to go." Lily's grip on Dawn tightened.

"I know, but we'll see Dawn again soon." Jack's eyes met Dawn's over his daughter's head. "Right?"

"Right," Dawn said quietly. "Very soon."

Jack carefully pulled his daughter away, and she instantly reached back for Dawn. The child's face showed longing. Jack's face, quickly masked, revealed an even deeper longing.

They left, and Dawn stood there, watching them go, with an expression Amy recognized, because she felt it every time she updated her spreadsheet and realized she was trying to organize her way into the kind of connection Dawn and Jack were building without any plan at all.

"The clue," Amy said, because someone needed to say something. "We found the next clue. It points to the old chapel."

"That's good." Dawn didn't look away from the door. "That's progress."

"Dawn—"

"I should help with costumes. They're a disaster, and the dress rehearsal is in two days." She walked away before Amy could say anything else about risk, staying, and building things that might break your heart.

William reappeared at Amy's side. "Ready to go?"

Yeah, let's go.

They walked back toward the town square in silence. Amy's mind was overwhelmed: the child's comment about marriage, Dawn's admission about staying, the weight of her own spreadsheet sitting in her phone's cloud storage like evidence of everything she was doing wrong.

"You're quiet," William said as they reached the square.

"Just thinking."

"About?"

"About how I'm really bad at this. The spontaneous, unplanned, let-things-happen approach to life. I watch Dawn just naturally connect with people, and Jack's daughter, and it looks so easy. But when I try, it feels like I'm performing a role I haven't memorized yet."

"Maybe you're trying too hard to get it right instead of just letting it happen."

"That's what everyone keeps telling me. 'Just let it happen, Amy. Stop trying to control everything, Amy. Trust the process, Amy.' But no one ever explains what happens when you let go and everything falls apart."

"Maybe it doesn't fall apart. Maybe it just looks different than you planned."

"Different like better, or different like disaster?"

"Different like alive."

Before she could respond, a voice called out across the square. "Amy? Amy Donovan?"

She turned, and her stomach dropped.

Peter Alexander stood near the gazebo, wearing an expensive coat and a relaxed smile. He looked exactly the same, sandy hair, kind eyes, and the posture of someone who'd been told in childhood that he had excellent posture and never forgot it.

He was also holding hands with a woman Amy didn't recognize. Petite, blonde, wearing an outfit that suggested she'd never accidentally spilled coffee on a historical photograph in her life.

"Oh my god, I thought that was you." Peter approached, bringing the blonde woman with him. "Amy, wow. How long has it been?"

"Three years." Her voice came out steadier than she felt. "Three years, two months."

"Right. Of course. Time flies." He gestured to the woman beside him. "This is Melissa. Melissa, this is Amy. We dated back when I lived here."

"Dated for eight months," Amy corrected, because precision mattered. "Until you ended things because I 'scheduled romance like a board meeting.'"

Peter's smile faltered. "I don't think I put it quite like that."

"You put it exactly like that. December eighth. Seven-fifteen PM. The Thai place on Oak Street."

"You remember the exact time?"

"I remember everything." She was aware of William beside her, quiet and watchful. Aware that this was humiliating. Aware that she was making it worse by being precise about her own humiliation.

"Well." Peter cleared his throat. "It's good to see you. You look great. Really great."

"Thank you."

"Are you visiting family for the holidays?"

"Among other things."

"Right, of course." He glanced at William, clearly trying to figure out their relationship. "And you're..."

"Working together," Amy said before William could answer. "On a historical project."

"That sounds perfect for you. You always loved organization and research." Peter's tone was fond, as if he were talking about a quirky habit rather than the reason he'd broken up with her. "I'm here visiting my parents for Christmas. Melissa and I are thinking about relocating here. She loves the small-town vibe of this town".

"That's great." Amy wanted to leave. Wanted to be literally anywhere else. "We should let you get back to your—"

"We should grab coffee while you're in town," Peter interrupted. "Catch up some. I'd love to hear what you've been up to."

Melissa's hand tightened on his arm. "Peter, we have lunch with your parents in twenty minutes."

"Right, yes." But he was still looking at Amy with something that painfully resembled interest. "But maybe later? Tomorrow?"

"I'm busy tomorrow." She wasn't. Her schedule was completely free. But she would light her spreadsheet on fire before having coffee with Peter and his girlfriend while he tested the waters to see if his ex was available as a backup plan.

Sure. No problem. Maybe I'll see you around town, then," he finally seemed to notice William's presence as more than just background noise. "Enjoy your historical project."

They left, Melissa practically dragging him toward the parking lot.

Amy stood there, knowing her hands were shaking, her throat was tight, and William was watching her with an expression she couldn't quite read.

"So," William said. "That was..."

"A mistake I made very carefully," Amy finished. "Peter Alexander. Accountant. Steady income. Family-oriented. Checked every box on my list of ideal partner qualities except the one where he loved me back."

"He seemed interested in reconnecting."

"He has a girlfriend."

"That doesn't always stop people."

"It should." She wrapped her arms around herself, suddenly cold despite her coat. "I should have known better. I did know better. But I was twenty-six and desperate to prove I could make a relationship work, so I ignored every sign that he was only with me because I was convenient and organized and wouldn't demand anything messy like actual emotional connection."

"Amy—"

You know what the worst part is? I made a spreadsheet for that relationship too. I tracked data like date quality, conversation topics, and how often we showed physical affection. Like if I could just optimize our compatibility, he'd eventually care about me the way I cared about him. But you can't spreadsheet someone into loving you." She laughed, but it came out wrong. "Turns out the universe has a sense of humor. Here I am, three years later, with seventeen names on a new list, still trying to organize my way to happiness."

William was quiet for a long moment. When he spoke, his voice was gentle. "For what it's worth, I think Peter's an idiot."

"Because I'm so delightful to be around? So spontaneous and easy and fun?"

"Because you're brilliant and determined and brave enough to keep trying even when you're terrified. And because you make me drink mediocre coffee and argue about cobblestones and sit on cold fountains eating hot chocolate like it's a normal thing to do." He took a step closer. "And because when you laugh, really laugh, not that careful professional sound, it's the best thing I've heard in three years."

She stared at him. "You're supposed to be making this easier, not harder."

"What's this?"

"This." She gestured between them. "Whatever this is. This... complication."

"You think I'm a complication?"

"You're on my list."

"I know."

"You're not supposed to be on my list. You're supposed to be the guy I work with on the Wish Box project, and then I leave, and we both move on with our lives."

"Supposed to be." He was still standing too close. "But what if things don't go the way they're supposed to?"

"Then everything falls apart."

"Or everything finally starts making sense."

She wanted to argue. Wanted to explain all the ways this was a terrible idea. Wanted to pull out her phone and show him the seventeen names who were safe and suitable and wouldn't make her feel like this, like she was standing on the edge of something vast and terrifying and possibly wonderful.

Instead, she heard herself say, "The chapel. We need to investigate the chapel tomorrow."

"Tomorrow," he agreed, and if he was disappointed by her retreat, he didn't show it. "I'll get the key."

"Good. That's good. Progress." She took a step back, creating proper distance. "I should go. I have a... I need to..."

"You need to sit with being uncomfortable."

"I need to update my schedule."

"Same thing."

She walked away before she could say anything else, before she could bridge the gap instead of widening it, before she could ask him what he meant about her laugh being the best thing he'd heard in three years.

Her phone buzzed as she reached the Evergreen Lodge.

Text from Dawn: *Saw you talking to Peter. You okay?*

Amy typed back: *Fine. Just an awkward ex encounter. No big deal.*

Another buzz. *And William looked like he wanted to punch something. Also no big deal?*

Amy stared at her phone, thinking about William standing beside her while Peter tested the waters. She reflected on how he had called her brilliant and brave. She also thought about children who could apparently see things that adults spend a lot of energy pretending don't exist.

She typed: *Everything's fine. See you at dinner.*

Then she opened her spreadsheet and stared at entry number four.

4. William Crane, 32, Historian and Business Owner

She should delete the note about his jawline. She should remove the observation about how he smelled like old books. She definitely should not add the new information about how he made her want to throw her entire carefully constructed plan into the nearest storm drain and just see what happened.

Instead, she added one line:

Note: Makes me laugh. Really laugh. This is a problem.

Then she closed the app and tried very hard not to calculate the probability that she was falling for someone who wasn't supposed to be part of the plan.

The number appeared anyway. Approximately 87%.

She was so screwed.

Chapter 6
William - December 7th

The chapel sat at the edge of town where Holly Falls gave way to forest, small and perfect and preserved just as they should be. William had the key because his grandfather had served on the historical preservation committee for thirty years, and some responsibilities get passed down whether you want them to or not.

He wanted this one.

The building was made of stone, gray and solid, with narrow windows of old glass that caught the afternoon light and turned it gold. The door was arched, heavy oak, with iron fixtures forged in 1848 by the town's original blacksmith. Inside, the space could hold maybe fifty people if they sat close together. Wooden pews worn smooth by generations of use. A simple altar with a white cloth. Candles in brass holders, unlit now but ready.

It smelled like old wood, candle wax, and something else William couldn't quite name.

Amy stood in the doorway, not quite stepping in, and her expression shifted from her usual focused efficiency to something more cautious. More uncertain.

William loved the chapel.

He had loved it since he was a boy, when he would sneak inside and sit in the third pew, waiting for the light to turn golden across the altar. Now he brought Amy here, not for romance, not really. For something quieter. A truth he couldn't name.

She ran her fingers along the wood, reverent.

"It's beautiful," she whispered.

He wanted to tell her she was, too. But his courage wasn't quite ready. "It is." He stepped inside, giving her space to follow at her own pace. "The town maintains it even though we only use it for special occasions now. Weddings, mostly. Sometimes, memorial services for old families who've been here since the beginning."

She moved inside slowly, like someone entering a museum. Her fingers brushed gently along the back of the nearest pew, and William noticed she touched the wood with respect.

"How old is it?"

Built in 1848, it is one of the first permanent structures in Holly Falls. The town founder and his wife were married here in 1849. Since then, it has become a tradition. Every founding family has had at least one wedding here.

"Including yours."

It wasn't a question. She'd been paying attention.

"My grandparents. My parents." He moved toward the altar, driven by habit, memory, or both. "I used to think I'd get married here too."

The words escaped before he could stop them, revealing more vulnerability than he intended to share. He waited for her to make a joke, deflect with ease, or shift the topic to the clue they were supposed to find.

Instead, she moved to the front and sat in the first pew, glancing up at the altar with an expression he couldn't quite understand.

"Used to think," she repeated. "Past tense."

"Plans change."

"Because of Ava?"

He should have been surprised she guessed, but he wasn't. Amy noticed everything, even when she acted like she didn't.

"Partly. Mostly because I realized the fantasy I had, walking down this aisle with someone who truly wanted to stay, building a life here, having kids who'd grow up the way I did, wasn't realistic. Or maybe it was realistic for some people, just not for me.

"Why not for you?"

He turned to look at her. She was watching him with those hazel eyes that change color depending on the light, and at this moment, they appeared more green than brown, soft, curious, and dangerously easy to get lost in.

"Because the women I meet either want to leave Holly Falls or just like the idea of Holly Falls without experiencing it firsthand. Ava wanted the look of a charming small-town boyfriend with a shop full of antiques and a family history she could share on social media. But she didn't want the real life — the quiet winters, the summers where everyone knows everyone, or the small scale of everything."

"She wanted the fantasy without the foundation."

"Exactly." He sat in the pew across the aisle from her, close enough to talk without the space feeling empty between them. "What about you? Have you been to many weddings?"

"Seventeen." She said it like she'd counted. She probably had. "Cousins, college friends, work colleagues. I've been to seventeen weddings, and I've never once believed one of them would actually last."

"That's bleak."

"That's realistic." But her voice was sad rather than cynical. "My parents divorced when I was twelve. One day they were married, the next day my dad was packing boxes and my mom was explaining that sometimes people fall out of love and it's nobody's fault."

"But you thought it was your fault."

She looked at him sharply. "How did you—"

"Because that's what kids do. They find ways to make everything their responsibility." He knew this because he'd watched his mother do it after his father left, watching her create elaborate explanations for why she hadn't been enough to make him stay. "What did you think you'd done wrong?"

Amy was quiet for a long moment. When she spoke, her voice was smaller than usual. Younger.

"I thought that if I had been better, smarter, quieter, more helpful, and less difficult, maybe he would've wanted to stay. Or perhaps if I had noticed sooner that something was wrong, I could have fixed it. I was really good at fixing things. I fixed my bike when the chain fell off, I fixed the toaster when it stopped working, I fixed the broken shelf in the garage. But I couldn't fix my parents' marriage because I didn't realize it was broken until it was already too late."

"Amy—"

"So I learned to pay attention. To see the cracks before they became breaks. To have a plan for every contingency. Because if I could just anticipate the problems, create the right systems, maintain the right standards, maybe I could prevent the next disaster." She looked down at her hands. "Except it turns out you can't prevent people from leaving just by being perfect. You can only exhaust yourself trying."

William crossed the aisle and sat next to her in the pew, close enough to brush shoulders, close enough to catch the scent of her citrus shampoo.

"You realize you don't have to earn this, right?" he murmured. "Being here. People wanting to know you. You don't have to be perfect to be worth someone's time."

Her throat worked. She didn't look at him. "Logically, I understand. Emotionally, though? I'm still twelve years old, convinced that if I had just been better, my dad wouldn't have left."

"He didn't leave because of you. Adults make decisions for adult reasons separate from their kids."

"I know. At least, I know it now. But the knowing doesn't fix the feeling."

He understood the difference. Knowing something intellectually and truly believing it deep down are entirely different. He had realized three years ago that Ava's departure wasn't a reflection of his worth, but he still felt the sting of "not enough" every time someone new arrived in town and looked around as if they were already planning their escape.

"For what it's worth," he said, "I believe you're more than enough just the way you are. Spreadsheets and all."

She turned to look at him then, and the expression on her face was so open and vulnerable that he felt something in his chest crack.

"You don't know me well enough to say that."

"It's clear to me you grabbed my arm in a basement because you were scared, but you went down with me because you said you would. It's obvious you document everything as it happens because you care about getting it right. You might turn off notifications when you want to be present, but I see you check your phone every seven minutes to calm yourself because the dark feels dangerous." He shifted slightly closer. "I love how you laugh like you're surprised by the sound. And I understand you're here in Holly Falls trying to organize your way to happiness because you don't believe anyone would choose you without a strategy."

"That's not—" Her voice broke. "That's too accurate."

"It's also wrong. The last part. I'd choose you without any strategy at all."

The silence that followed was so complete it let him hear her breath catch, see her pupils dilate, and feel the space between them shrink, even though neither of them had moved.

"William—"

He reached up and tucked a strand of hair behind her ear that had fallen from her ponytail. Her skin was soft under his fingers, and she went still, watching him with those shifting hazel eyes.

"I'm going to kiss you," he said, giving her time to object, time to pull away, time to do anything except keep looking at him like he'd just said something that made sense of the world.

"Okay," she whispered.

He leaned in slowly, giving her every chance to change her mind, watching as her eyes fluttered closed, feeling her breath against his lips…

A chime sliced the stillness.

Not a shrill sound. Just a soft, melodic reminder. But it might as well have been a fire alarm.

Amy flinched. "Oh no," she breathed, scrambling for her phone. Her fingers missed the screen twice before she finally silenced it. It was too late.

William had already seen the words flash across:

Candidate Review: 2PM.

The moment, golden and open and rare, collapsed in on itself.

Amy's mouth opened, apology halfway to her lips, but he was already pulling back, both physically and mentally. His eyes shuttered, and the careful distance of years slid back into place like armor.

It hurt to recognize the look.

"William, wait, please. The alarm, it's not what you think—"

"What do I think, Amy?" His voice wasn't sharp, but it was cooler than before. A fraction quieter. "I think while I was about to kiss you, you were on a timer to compare me to a spreadsheet of eligible strangers."

She shook her head quickly. "No. God, no. I set it before. I just forgot to—"

"To cancel the schedule for screening someone else while we were, what? Having a moment?" He offered a smile with no warmth behind it.

"Yes. No. I don't know. I didn't expect any of this. You weren't supposed to be…"

She stopped herself. Too late.

"Weren't supposed to be what?"

Amy's throat worked, her words tangled in too many truths. "Real."

William exhaled heavily, a mixture of a laugh and a sigh. "Well, I'm here. Not in your spreadsheet. Not part of your contingency plan. But real, nonetheless."

She looked distressed, like someone watching something delicate slip away. "Please don't read it that way. My alarm wasn't about comparing you. It was about protecting myself."

That landed.

He didn't answer immediately.

Then, softer, "I get needing protection. I do. I've just spent so long trying not to want things I couldn't trust, I forgot how much it could hurt to want them."

Amy's voice dropped. "I didn't mean to hurt you."

"I know."

They stood there in the stillness, the chapel walls echoing silence louder than bells.

Then, in a quiet voice: "I wanted to kiss you, William. I still do. But I'm scared I'll mess this up, just like everything else I try to control too tightly."

His jaw tightened, but not in anger. In understanding.

He reached out and gently took the phone from her hand. Turned it over. Set it face down on the pew.

"Then maybe the first step," he said, "is not giving fear an alarm."

William walked to the altar, found the inscription he'd noticed when they first arrived, carved into the wooden cover of the old registry that sat there. He opened it carefully and turned to the first page where someone had written in elaborate script.

"The clue's here," he said. "In the registry."

After putting her phone away, Amy moved closer and took out her camera, but her hands were trembling slightly.

He read the inscription aloud: "'Where promises were spoken and hearts were bound, where water flows beneath the sacred ground, seek the bridge where two paths meet and part, where the founder spoke his steadfast heart.'"

"The footbridge," Amy said, her voice steadier now that they were back on task. "Over Holly Creek. You mentioned the town founder proposed there."

102

"He did. Built the bridge himself, carried his bride across it when the creek flooded that spring, proposed on the far side.

"That's very romantic."

"He was a romantic and impractical, according to historical accounts. He married a woman whom half the settlement thought was too educated for a frontier town. She proved them wrong by designing the town's water system and teaching at the school for forty years."

"She sounds like someone who would've had a spreadsheet."

She probably did. The 1840s equivalent, anyway." He carefully closed the registry and put it back in its place. "Amy—"

"That alarm wasn't about you, she said hurriedly. "It was about me being scared that if I didn't follow the plan, if I just let myself feel what my emotions are telling me, I would end up like I always do, alone and wondering what I did wrong."

"What are you feeling?"

She opened her mouth, then closed it. She looked at him with those shifting hazel eyes and something that might have been panic.

"Every part of me wants to kiss you," she said finally. "But my gut says that's a terrible idea because you're going to realize I'm too much work and too high maintenance and too fundamentally broken to be worth the effort."

"Amy—"

"And I realize that's my wound talking. I understand that intellectually I'm catastrophizing, but knowing that doesn't make the fear go away," she took a breath. "So yes, I had an alarm set to review candidate profiles because having a plan makes me feel safe even when the plan is clearly not working. But that doesn't mean I want anyone on that list; it just means I'm unsure how to function without some kind of safety net."

He understood safety nets. He had built his own from cynicism, low expectations, and cautious distance from anyone who might leave.

"What if we tried something?" he suggested.

"What?"

"What if, for the next week, we both try letting go of our safety nets? You turn off your reminders and close your spreadsheet. I stop assuming every woman I meet is going to leave. We just see what happens."

"That's terrifying."

"Probably."

"What if it doesn't work?"

"Then we'll have learned something."

"What if it does work?"

"Then we'll have learned something better."

She gazed at him for a long moment, her face shifting between fear, hope, and what might have been determination.

Then she opened her phone, navigated to her settings, and started turning off alarms.

He watched as notification after notification was silenced. Reminders disappeared. Color-coded blocks on her calendar turned gray.

"I'm maintaining my current work commitments," she said. "I'm not completely abandoning structure."

"I wouldn't expect you to."

"But the candidate reviews, the strategic networking time, the research hours..." She turned off the last alarm. "Gone."

"How does that feel?"

"Like I'm free-falling," she looked up at him. "But also like maybe that's not the worst thing."

They exited the chapel together, William carefully locking the door behind them. The December afternoon was chilly, with the sun already beginning its descent toward the horizon, and the trees stood bare and dark against the pale sky.

Amy stopped him halfway down the path.

"That alarm," she said. "In the chapel. It really wasn't about you."

"I realize that."

"Do you? Because you looked hurt, and I don't want you to think I was comparing you to some list of qualifications while we were about to—" She stopped, flushed. "While we were having a moment."

"Were we having a moment?"

"We were experiencing many moments. A whole collection of moments. Some of which were very good before I ruined them with poor alarm management."

He smiled despite himself. "Poor alarm management. Is that what we're calling it?"

"I'm calling it a temporary lapse in judgment regarding notification settings. You can call it whatever you want."

"I'm calling it human. You're allowed to be uncertain and scared and to have safety nets that don't make sense to anyone else. You're allowed to have alarms go off at terrible times because you're still figuring out how to let go of the plan."

"You're being very understanding about this."

"I'm being honest. I've spent three years using cynicism as armor so I wouldn't have to risk my emotions. I don't get to judge you for using spreadsheets."

They arrived at the outskirts of town where the path intersected with the main road. Amy pulled out her phone again, and William watched as she opened an app he recognized, her spreadsheet application.

She navigated to her candidate database, scrolled through entries, her expression unreadable.

Then she closed the app without making any changes.

"I'm not deleting it," she said. "Not yet. But I'm not looking at it either."

"That's progress."

"That's terrifying." She smiled slightly. "Tomorrow we'll investigate the footbridge and find the next clue. Let's continue this entirely professional working relationship that definitely doesn't involve moments in chapels."

"Definitely doesn't."

"Good. That's settled." She started walking toward the town square, then stopped and turned back. "William?"

"Yeah?"

"Thank you. For saying I don't have to earn this. Even if I don't believe you yet."

"You will eventually."

"How do you know?"

"Because you're brave enough to turn off the alarms. That's harder than it looks."

She nodded, something shifting in her expression, and walked away.

William stood there watching her go, observing how she moved with purpose, even when her purpose was simply walking home, and felt something in his chest he'd been trying hard not to acknowledge.

He was falling for her.

For the woman with the spreadsheet, alarms, and color-coded calendar blocks. For the woman who grabbed his arm in basements, documented everything immediately, and believed she had to be perfect to be worthy of love.

He was falling for Amy Donovan, and she'd just turned off her alarms and closed her spreadsheet without deleting it, which felt like the bravest thing he'd seen in years.

Tomorrow they'd search the footbridge, find another clue, and keep pretending this was just a professional collaboration, not something much more complicated.

But tonight, he'd let himself acknowledge the truth:

He'd already chosen her, spreadsheet and all.

And he had no idea if that made him brave or just another kind of fool.

Chapter 7
Amy - December 9th

The footbridge over Holly Creek appeared older than it seemed from a distance. Up close, Amy could observe the weathered wooden planks, the iron railings that had been repaired and reinforced over the years, and the careful upkeep that kept something built in 1847 functional in 2024.

William ran his hand along the railing with the same reverence he reserved for historic objects that had survived against all odds.

"The town founder built this himself," he said. "Jonathan Holloway. He was a methodical man, according to the journals. Planned everything. Measured twice, cut once. Built this bridge during the spring thaw of 1848 because he needed a reliable way to reach the other side of the creek."

"Practical," Amy said, taking photographs of the bridge's construction from multiple angles.

"Very. Except he fell apart completely when he met Sarah Greene. She arrived in Holly Falls with her father in the fall of 1848; they were teachers hired by the settlement to start a school. Jonathan took one look at her and apparently forgot how to form complete sentences."

"That's very romantic."

"It's very human. He spent three months trying to muster the courage to speak to her. Finally, in January 1849, he gathered enough nerve to ask if he could escort her across the creek. It had frozen over, and the bridge was slippery."

"Let me guess. He proposed on the other side."

"He proposed in the middle, got down on one knee right there—" William pointed to the center of the bridge. "On ice, in January, with the entire town watching from both banks because word had gotten out that Jonathan Holloway was going to make his move."

Amy smiled despite herself. "Did she say yes?"

"She said yes. They were married in the chapel six weeks later. They had four children, ran the school together for thirty years, and according to every account, constantly annoyed each other while loving one another more."

"Annoyed each other constantly?"

She believed his planning was too much. He believed her spontaneity was too risky. But they made it work because they decided the irritation was worth it.

Amy looked at him, at the way the winter light caught in his hair, at the small smile playing at the corner of his mouth. "Are you trying to tell me something?"

"I'm telling you about the town founder's marriage."

"Right. The town founder who was methodical and fell apart when he encountered someone unexpected."

"Exactly." His smile widened. "Completely unrelated to anything happening in present day."

She laughed, that surprised sound he seemed to pull from her without effort. "You're not subtle."

"I'm a historian. Subtlety isn't the job."

He moved toward the far end of the bridge, crouching to examine the base of the railing. Amy followed, her camera ready, trying not to overthink about methodical men who fell apart for the right person.

"There's ice under here," William said, gesturing to the spot where the creek ran below. "It freezes solid most winters. When I was eight, I fell through. Right there." He pointed to a spot maybe ten feet from where they stood.

"That sounds terrifying."

"It was. Also extremely cold." He touched the scar through his left eyebrow, the gesture automatic. "Hit my head on the ice going down. My grandfather pulled me out, but not before I'd gotten a pretty good gash."

Amy moved closer, studying the scar she had noticed before but never asked about. A thin white line cut through the dark hair of his eyebrow, which was raised.

"Can I—" She stopped, suddenly self-conscious. "Can I touch it?"

He went very still. "Yeah."

She reached up slowly, giving him time to change his mind, and lightly traced the scar with her fingertip. His skin was warm despite the December cold, and she felt him take a careful breath.

"Does it hurt?" she asked.

"Not anymore."

"It's a good story, though. Falling through ice, grandfather's rescue, permanent scar. Very dramatic."

"I was eight. Everything was dramatic."

"Some things are worth being dramatic about." She let her hand linger there, her fingers gentle on his face, aware that they were standing very close together on a bridge in broad daylight where anyone could see them.

She should step back. This was too much, too intimate, too public.

She didn't step back.

"Amy—" His voice was rough.

"I'm looking for the clue," she said, which was a blatant lie. She was watching him, noting how his eyes had darkened and noticing how carefully he was not moving, even though she was touching his face in the middle of a public bridge.

"The clue," he repeated.

"Yes. The historical clue. About vows and promises." She dropped her hand, stepped back, and created the proper distance that should have existed all along. "We should search the railing. That's where inscriptions would be carved."

"Right. The railing."

They searched quietly now, a comfortable silence that came from working together enough times to develop a rhythm. Amy took the near side, William the far side, both of them running their hands along the wood and iron, looking for anything that seemed deliberately placed rather than naturally weathered.

"Here." William's voice carried across the bridge. "There's text carved into the railing. Very faint, but it's there."

Amy moved to his side and took out her camera. The carving was faint, worn smooth by decades of weather and handling, but she could still make out letters in an old-fashioned script.

William read aloud: "'Where two paths cross and promises were made, where the methodical heart was unafraid, seek now where winter's abundance is shared, where giving is free and all souls are cared.'"

"Where abundance is shared freely," Amy murmured, already processing. "Charity. Donations. The Christmas market?"

"The market has donation boxes for the community fund. Everything collected goes to families who need help with heating costs, food, medical bills." William was already walking toward the town end of the bridge. "If the clue is about abundance being shared, that's where we'll find it."

They walked together toward the town square, where the Christmas market had been set up the week before. White tents lined the edges, with vendors selling everything from hand-knit scarves and homemade preserves to wooden toys carved by local artisans. The air smelled of cinnamon, pine, and roasted chestnuts.

It was crowded. Very crowded. People everywhere, moving between booths, calling out greetings, children running with the kind of chaos that comes from too much sugar and holiday excitement.

Amy's instinct was to catalog the chaos, plan the most efficient route through the market, and develop a system to avoid the densest crowds.

Instead, she simply walked alongside William, letting him lead while she observed her surroundings. She noticed how Mrs. Peterson waved at them from the baked goods booth. She also noticed Michael Watson calling out, "Looking good, you two!" from the coffee cart. And she observed how people watched them with knowing smiles and curious expressions.

The way William reached over and took her hand.

Not dramatically. Not with any announcement. Just slipped his fingers through hers as if it were the most natural thing in the world.

Amy's first instinct was to pull away. They were in public, and everyone was watching. This would become town gossip within the hour.

Her second instinct was to hold on tighter.

She compromised by not pulling away but also developing a sudden fascination with the nearest vendor's holiday ornament display.

"Everyone's staring," she said.

"Small town. Everyone stares at everything."

"They're staring at us. Together. Holding hands."

"Does that bother you?"

"I don't know." She risked a glance up at him. "Should it?"

"Only if you don't want people to know you're willing to be seen with the town historian who lectures about cobblestones."

"I've made peace with the cobblestone lectures."

"Have you made peace with hand-holding in public?"

She reflected on it. On her spreadsheet with its seventeen names and compatibility probabilities. On the alarms she had turned off two days ago. On the way her hand felt in his, warm, solid, and somehow right despite making no logical sense.

"I'm working on it," she said.

"Good enough."

They found the donation box in the center of the market, a large wooden chest painted with festive designs and labeled COMMUNITY FUND in cheerful letters. People were dropping in cash, checks, gift cards, whatever they could spare to help neighbors in need.

William examined the construction as he approached it. "This is the original chest. Built in 1952 when the Christmas market first started. They restore it every year, but the base structure remains the same."

"So the clue would be somewhere on the original structure."

Probably inside, under the donation slot," he looked around, took note of the crowd, then called out, "Hey, Marcus? Can we borrow this for ten minutes? Historical society business.

A man in a thick coat and volunteer badge waved them on. "Take your time. I'll let people know where to put donations while you're examining it."

William and Amy carried the chest to a quieter corner near the gazebo. It wasn't heavy, since most of the donations had already been collected, but it was awkward, and they had to work together to maneuver it without dropping it.

Amy knelt beside it and peered into the donation slot. "There's something carved on the inside. I can see text, but I can't read it without better light."

William pulled out his phone, turned on the flashlight, and angled it so she could see.

The carving was clear, protected from weather by being inside the chest: "'Where knowledge is kept and stories told, where the past speaks and secrets unfold, seek the keeper of words and the guardian of time, where truth lives in chapters and pages and rhyme.'"

"The library," Amy said immediately. "Where stories are preserved. That's the town library."

"Specifically, the historical archives section." William was already making notes in his small notebook. "The reference to 'keeper of words and guardian of time' suggests the archives rather than the general collection."

"Do you have access to those archives?"

"I have access to most of the town's historical collections. The librarian is—" He paused. "Actually, you know her. Joan Morrison. She's the director."

Amy's stomach dropped. "Joan Morrison who promoted her niece over more qualified candidates? That Joan Morrison?"

"I didn't know you knew her."

"She's the reason I have so much free time for clue-hunting. She cut my hours at the library in Pleasant Valley down to almost nothing." Amy stood, brushed off her knees. "This should be fun."

"She's territorial about the archives, but if I ask nicely—"

"William! Amy!"

They both turned to see Dawn waving from a booth selling handmade ornaments. Jack stood next to her, Lily perched on his hip, and the three of them looked so much like a family that Amy felt a tug in her chest.

"Come see!" Dawn called out. "Lily made an ornament, and she wants to show you."

They approached, still holding hands, and Amy watched Jack notice, saw his eyebrows lift again, and observed him hide a smile.

"Look!" Lily held up a wooden ornament painted with lively, abstract swirls of red and green. "I made a tree!"

"That's a beautiful tree," Amy said seriously. "Very artistic."

"Dawn helped." Lily beamed at Dawn with the simple adoration only five-year-olds can show. "Miss Dawn is good at painting."

"Dawn is our friend," Jack corrected gently, emphasis on friend in a way that made Dawn's smile falter a little.

Amy saw it, the flicker of panic, the instinct to run, and how Dawn's hand clenched the ornament she was holding.

"Can I borrow my sister for a minute?" Amy asked Jack.

"Of course." He took the ornament from Dawn, his fingers brushing hers, his expression neutral even though Amy could see the hope beneath.

Amy pulled Dawn aside, into the narrow space between booths where they could talk without an audience.

"You're panicking," Amy said without preamble.

"I'm not panicking. I'm just—"

"You're panicking because Jack said 'our friend' and Lily called you 'Miss Dawn' like you're a permanent fixture and you're realizing this isn't just a fun temporary thing anymore."

Dawn deflated. "Is it that obvious?"

"Only to someone who recognizes the fear because she's felt it herself."

"I'm falling for him," Dawn said. "For both of them. And I don't know what to do with that because I don't stay. I don't build. I just visit and move on before it gets complicated."

"Except it's already complicated."

"Exactly." Dawn wrapped her arms around herself. "And the terrifying part is that I want to stay. I want to see where this goes. But what if I stay and it doesn't work out? What if I stay and he realizes I'm not cut out for this, for being someone's partner, for being in a kid's life, for small-town permanence?"

"What if you stay and it does work out?"

"That's even more terrifying."

Amy knew that all too well. Success was more intimidating than failure because success meant you had something to lose.

"Don't run just because it's scary," she said. "Run if you genuinely don't want this. Run if it's wrong. But don't run just because it's unfamiliar."

Dawn looked at her with something that might have been surprise. "That's good advice."

"I'm full of good advice I don't follow myself."

"You're holding hands with William in public even though your spreadsheet shows someone more suitable with a higher likelihood."

"I turned off the spreadsheet."

"You what?"

Two days ago. Turned off all the alarms, closed the app, and decided to try being present instead of just going through the motions. Amy squeezed Dawn's hand. "And it's terrifying, but it's also the first thing I've done in years that feels real instead of performed."

Dawn studied her face. "You really like him."

I really do. Which makes no sense because he's not on the list, he's not suitable based on any of my criteria, and he makes me want to throw all my organizational systems into the creek and see what happens.

"That sounds healthy."

"That sounds insane."

Same thing sometimes," Dawn said as she glanced back at Jack, who was showing Lily how to tie string through the ornament so it could hang on a tree. "What if I mess this up?"

"What if you don't?"

"You're annoyingly optimistic today."

"I'm annoyingly terrified and pretending it's optimism."

They walked back to the booth together. Jack looked up as they approached, his expression cautious, and Amy noticed the exact moment he chose not to push, not to ask what they'd discussed, not to make Dawn feel trapped by expectations.

"Lily wants to know if you'll help her make another ornament," he said to Dawn. "I'm not artistic enough in her opinion."

"You're plenty artistic," Dawn said, but she was already moving closer, already reaching for the paint brushes, already choosing to stay for one more moment instead of running.

Amy caught Jack's eye. He mouthed "thank you," and she nodded, a silent understanding passing between them, two people watching someone they care about learn to be brave.

William touched her elbow. "We should return the donation box before Marcus thinks we've stolen the community fund."

They carried it back together, put it in its place, and Amy felt hesitant to let go of the task that gave them a reason to stay close in public.

"Tomorrow," William said. "The library. We'll need to coordinate with Joan about accessing the archives."

"I can handle Joan."

"She's not your biggest fan."

"She's not my biggest fan because I wouldn't tolerate her nepotism. But I can remain professional for the sake of the Wish Box project."

"I don't doubt it." He kept holding her hand, and she had stopped noticing the people watching. Or she was choosing not to care. One of those.

"Amy! Hey, Amy!"

She turned, and her stomach sank for the second time that day.

Peter was walking toward them, with Melissa trailing behind, looking uncomfortable. He had that smile on his face, the kind that usually meant he was about to suggest an activity he'd already decided they would do regardless of her opinion.

"I've been hoping I'd run into you again," Peter said as he reached them. He glanced at William, at their joined hands, and a flicker of emotion crossed his face. "Enjoying the market?"

"We're working," Amy said flatly.

"Right, the historical project. That's great. Really great." He rocked back on his heels. "Listen, I wanted to apologize for the other day. I think I came across as—"

"As someone testing the waters with an ex while dating someone else?" Amy supplied.

Melissa's expression suggested this was not the first time she'd heard something like this.

Peter's smile faltered. "That's not… I was just being friendly."

"No, you were being inappropriate. And honestly, Peter, you need to grow up." Amy felt William's hand tighten on hers, supportive. "You don't get to date someone—" she nodded at Melissa, "—while simultaneously testing whether your ex is available as a backup plan."

"That's not what I was doing."

"That's exactly what you were doing. And for the record, I wouldn't consider you even if you were the last man on earth. You broke up with me because I treated romance like a board meeting, and then you spent three years dating women who also scheduled things because that's what organized adults do. So either you were lying about why you ended it, or you've just realized that having someone who plans dates and remembers birthdays is actually convenient."

"Amy—"

"I'm not finished. We dated for eight months. You knew who I was—how I was—someone who needs structure, plans, and color-coded calendars to feel safe. And instead of accepting that or helping me feel safe enough to let go sometimes, you made me feel broken. So no, Peter. I'm not interested in coffee. I'm not interested in 'catching up.' I'm not interested in being your backup plan while you decide if Melissa is worth committing to."

Melissa was looking at Peter with an expression that hinted they would have a talk later.

Peter opened his mouth. Closed it. After a moment managed, "I should go."

"Yes," Amy agreed. "You should."

He left, Melissa following with one last glance over her shoulder that could have been gratitude or might have been horror. Amy wasn't sure which.

"Wow," William said.

"Was that too much?"

"That was perfect. I especially liked the part about being the last man on earth."

"I've been wanting to say that for three years."

"How does it feel?"

"Good, really good." She looked up at him. "Thank you for not jumping in. I know he was being obnoxious."

"You were handling it. I figured you'd let me know if you needed backup."

"I liked having you there anyway. As support."

"Anytime." He squeezed her hand. "For the record, I think Peter's an idiot for multiple reasons, but mainly for making you feel like organization and planning make you broken rather than capable."

"You're just saying that because you benefit from my organizational skills for this project."

"I'm saying that because it's true. You're not broken, Amy. You're just scared. There's a difference."

She wanted to argue. She wanted to point out all the ways she was clearly too much work. But standing there in the Christmas market, holding hands with a man who lectured about cobblestones and thought her spreadsheets were understandable rather than pathological, she couldn't quite bring herself to believe the old story.

"Tomorrow," she said instead. "The library. We'll find the next clue and continue this absolutely professional working relationship."

"Absolutely professional."

"With no hand-holding or intimate moments."

"Definitely not."

"Good. That's settled."

They walked back through the market together, still holding hands, and Amy tried not to calculate the odds that she was falling for him.

The number appeared anyway. Ninety-four percent.

She was screwed. So screwed. But maybe, possibly, the good kind of screwed.

Chapter 8
William - December 11th

The Pleasant Valley Library closed to the public at six o'clock on weekdays, which was why William had suggested they arrive at six-fifteen. Joan Morrison was predictable; she left at 6:05 every single day, locked her office, and drove home to her perfectly scheduled evening routine.

William had his own key to the archives, a courtesy given to the town historian that remained even after Joan took over as director and clearly saw his access requests as "disruptive to established procedures."

Amy had been quiet when he'd explained they'd be going after hours. He'd expected protest; she was the one with the organizational principles, the one who followed rules and created systems. Instead, she'd said, "Good. I don't want to deal with Joan anyway."

Now they stood in the library's basement archives room, surrounded by boxes and filing cabinets and the familiar smell of old paper that William had loved since childhood.

Amy moved through the space with careful caution, not touching anything yet, just observing. She'd brought her notebook and camera, her bag packed with the same precision as always, but she seemed more relaxed than she had a week ago. Less brittle. More present.

"Your notation system," she said, gesturing to the labels on the filing cabinets. "It's not Dewey Decimal."

"It's organized chronologically within each category. Town records, property deeds, meeting minutes, photographs, each is arranged by date of origin rather than by subject.

"That's actually brilliant. If you're researching a specific time period, you can gather everything relevant at once instead of searching through multiple classification systems.

"That's the idea." He was ridiculously pleased that she understood. Most people's eyes glazed over when he tried to explain his archival methodology. "My grandfather developed it. I've just maintained it."

"He taught you everything, didn't he? The shop, the archives, the preservation techniques."

"He taught me that history matters. That the small details, the everyday records, the ordinary lives, are what tell you who people were. The big events get remembered automatically. It's the small stuff that needs protecting."

She was looking at him with an expression he couldn't quite read. Not pity, exactly. More like recognition.

"That's why you stayed here," she said. "After college, after you could have gone anywhere. You stayed to finish what he started."

"I stayed because I wanted to. This work, this place, it's where I belong."

"Even when people leave?"

"Especially then."

He moved to the filing cabinet labeled PHOTOGRAPHS 1990-2000, pulled out a box, and started sorting through it, looking for images of the old schoolhouse that had been turned into a museum in 1998.

Amy came to stand beside him, close enough that he could smell that citrus shampoo, close enough that their shoulders almost touched.

"Is that you?" She pointed at a photograph near the top of the stack.

William's stomach dropped.

The photo captured the annual town barbecue, probably about four years ago. He stood near the food tables with Ava beside him, her hand on his arm, both of them smiling at the camera. She wore a sundress that he remembered she'd bought specifically because it looked "authentically small-town." He wore the expression of someone who thought he'd finally found what he'd been searching for.

"That's me," he said, voice neutral. "And Ava."

"She's beautiful."

"She was. Is. I assume she still is."

Amy picked up the photograph and studied it with the same attention she gave to historical documents. "You look happy."

"I thought I was."

"But you weren't?"

He should deflect. Change the subject. Get back to searching for the clue they were supposed to be finding. Instead, he found himself saying, "I was happy with the idea of what we could be. Turns out she was only happy with the idea of what I represented."

"What did you represent?"

Authenticity. Small-town charm. The appeal of dating a historian who lived above an antique shop and could tell you the history of any building in town." He took the photo from her and examined it closely. "She loved the Instagram version of my life. The curated story she could tell her friends. She didn't love the actual life, the quiet winters, the everyone-knows-everyone atmosphere, the fact that my idea of excitement was finding a well-preserved property deed from 1873."

"How long did it last?"

"Six months. Long enough for me to believe it was real. Short enough that when the DC job offer came and she admitted she'd been 'playing house,' I felt like an idiot for not noticing it sooner."

"You weren't an idiot. You were hopeful."

"Same thing, sometimes." He put the photo back into the box and struggled to find the words to explain what Ava's leaving had done to him. "I thought she saw me. The actual me, the guy who lectures about cobblestones, gets excited about archival notation systems, and wants to spend his life preserving things most people don't even notice. But she saw a character in a story she was telling herself. And when the story became boring, she left."

The silence that followed felt heavy. William kept his eyes on the filing cabinet, rearranging photographs he'd already sorted, because looking at Amy while discussing his wound felt too vulnerable.

"I understand that," Amy said. "Different manifestations, same fear. You're afraid of being someone's temporary aesthetic. I'm afraid of being someone's permanent obligation. You worry they'll leave when you stop being interesting. I worry they'll leave when I can't maintain perfection."

He turned to look at her. She was staring at the photograph in the box, her expression distant.

"Peter made you feel like an obligation," he guessed.

Peter made me feel like a project that wasn't going as planned. Like if I could just be less high-maintenance, less structured, less myself, then maybe he'd want to stay. She looked up at him. "But the thing is, I couldn't be less me. I tried. I turned off alarms, I stopped making lists, I pretended spontaneity was fun instead of terrifying. And he still left because he didn't want me; he wanted the convenient parts of me without the complicated parts."

"Ava wanted the aesthetic parts without the boring parts."

"So we both learned the same lesson. We're not enough as we are."

"Or," William said, "we learned that we were looking in the wrong places."

"What's the right place?"

"I'm not sure. But I think it's somewhere that doesn't need you to turn off alarms or me to be more interesting. Somewhere that prefers the real, boring, complicated version instead of the polished story."

She was silent for a long moment. Then she said, "I came here with a plan. To Holly Falls. I had a whole strategy for meeting someone suitable and building something functional before Christmas."

"I know. Dawn mentioned it."

"Right. Of course she did." Amy laughed, but it sounded pained. "I had seventeen names. Compatibility probabilities. Risk assessments. A timeline for relationship milestones. It was pathological and desperate and completely serious."

"What happened to the plan?"

"I met you," she said simply, as if that explained everything. "And suddenly, the plan stopped making sense. The timelines felt random. The compatibility metrics seemed pointless. Because none of the seventeen people on my list made me want to sit on cold fountains drinking hot chocolate, search through dusty basements for historical clues, or turn off all my alarms and see what happens."

"Amy—"

I'm not deleting the spreadsheet," she said quickly. "I can't. Not yet. Because what if this doesn't work? What if you realize I'm too much work, or I realize I can't function without structure, or we're just not compatible in some fundamental way I haven't considered yet? I need to know I have options. I need to know there's a backup plan."

"I understand that."

"Do you? Because you look disappointed."

"I'm not disappointed. I'm terrified." He took a step closer to her, close enough that the filing cabinet pressed against his back, close enough that she had to look up to meet his eyes. "I'm terrified because I spent three years building walls just to avoid feeling what I'm feeling right now. And you're standing here telling me you came to my town with a list of suitable bachelors, and I'm not on that list, and I still can't make myself care because all I can think about is the way you laugh when I make terrible historical puns and the way you grabbed my arm in the basement and the way you told Peter Alexander he was the last man on earth you'd consider."

"William—"

"So keep your spreadsheet. Keep your backup plans. Keep whatever safety nets you need to feel okay taking a risk on this. But know that I'm taking the same risk. And I'm just as terrified as you are."

The silence between them felt charged, heavy with everything they weren't quite saying.

Amy cleared her throat. "We should find the clue."

"We should."

Neither of them moved.

"In the town charter," she said. "That's where the riddle would be hidden, right? The official founding documents?"

"Right." He forced himself to step back, create proper distance, and focus on the task instead of the way she was looking at him. "Town charter is in the temperature-controlled cabinet. This way."

He led her to the far corner where the most valuable documents were stored in a specialized cabinet that controlled humidity and temperature.

The town charter was in a protective sleeve, the parchment yellowed but still readable, with the signatures of the founding families clearly visible at the bottom.

William opened the sleeve carefully, lifted the document to the light.

There, along the bottom margin, almost hidden unless you knew where to look: text in the same ornate script as the other clues.

Amy pulled out her camera and snapped photos from multiple angles while William read aloud: "'Where young minds are shaped and futures are born, where knowledge is taught from night until morn, seek the place where children learn to see, the schoolhouse of old where wisdom runs free.'"

"The old schoolhouse," Amy said, already taking notes. "The one that's now the historical museum."

That's the one. Built in 1852, it served as the school until 1963 when they built the new one. The town converted it to a museum in 1998 to preserve the building and create a space for historical exhibits.

"Do you have access?"

"I have keys to most of the historical buildings in town. Comes with being the town historian." He checked his watch. "It's almost seven. We could go now if you want. The museum is closed to the public, but we can access it for research purposes."

"After hours research. We're making a habit of this."

"Is that a problem?"

"No." She gave a small smile. "It's nice. Avoiding crowds. Working when everything's quiet."

"And avoiding Joan Morrison?"

"That too."

They packed up their materials, locked the archive room behind them, and stepped out into the December evening. The temperature had dropped with the sun, cold enough that their breath fogged in the air.

The museum was just four blocks away, a small brick building with the distinctive charm of nineteenth-century educational architecture. William unlocked the door and turned on the lights.

The space was carefully preserved, with original desks arranged in neat rows, a teacher's desk at the front, and a chalkboard with the alphabet still written in neat script. Display cases lined the walls, showcasing artifacts from Holly Falls' early days: tools, clothing, photographs, and letters.

"It's beautiful," Amy said, moving through the space with her camera. "Like stepping back in time."

"That's the idea." William lit the old oil lamps sitting on the teacher's desk; the museum kept them fueled for authenticity, even though they also had modern lighting. The golden glow filled the room, warm and inviting.

"The clue would be in an exhibit," he said. "Something about wisdom or knowledge or teaching."

They searched together, moving from one case to another, searching for anything that appeared deliberately arranged rather than casually displayed.

"Here." Amy stopped in front of a case displaying old textbooks and writing implements. "There's text carved into the frame. Very small, but it's there."

William stepped closer, squinting at the tiny letters carved along the bottom of the display case frame. They were nearly invisible, worn smooth by time and countless hands touching the case.

"'Where light guides the weary home,'" he read. "That's all it says. Just that one line."

"The lighthouse," Amy said immediately. "The decorative one on the ridge overlooking the valley. That's where the next clue will be."

"Probably." But he was distracted by how close she was standing, by the way the lamplight caught in her hair, and by the fact that they were alone in a museum after hours, and she'd just told him she made her want to abandon her carefully planned scheme.

"William." Her voice was quiet.

"Yeah?"

"We're standing very close together."

"I noticed."

"Is that intentional?"

"Probably."

She fully turned to face him, and they were just inches apart, with the display case behind her and him blocking her in without actually touching her.

"This is a bad idea," she said, but she didn't move away.

"Terrible idea."

"We're working together. Professionally."

"Very professionally."

"And I'm still scared I'll mess this up. That I'll be too much work or not enough fun or some combination of both that makes you realize this was a mistake."

"Then we'll mess it up together," he said, echoing his words from the chapel. "I'm not expecting perfect, Amy. I'm just asking for real."

Her eyes searched his face. "I don't know if I know how to do real without planning it first."

"So don't plan it. Just let it happen."

"That's terrifying."

"I know."

He could see her processing, could almost hear the calculations running through her mind, and could watch her struggle between the instinct to retreat and the desire to stay.

Then she slightly rose on her toes, closing the distance, and he understood her choice.

He leaned down, his hand coming up to cup her face, his thumb brushing her cheekbone, and he could feel her breath against his lips, could see her eyes fluttering closed...

A door slammed somewhere in the building.

They both jumped apart.

"Hello?" A voice called out. "Somebody in here? Building's supposed to be locked."

"It's William Crane," William called back, his voice rougher than intended. "Historical society. We're just finishing up some research."

"Oh. Right. Okay." The janitor, Bob something, William couldn't remember his last name, appeared in the doorway holding a mop. "Didn't know anyone was here. I'll just... I'll come back."

"We're done," Amy said quickly, already gathering her bag, her face flushed. "We found what we needed. We should go."

"Right. Yes. Going." William grabbed his notebook, started turning off the oil lamps with unsteady hands.

Bob watched them with a knowing look, as if he'd clearly interrupted something, then turned and disappeared into the hallway with a barely contained smile.

"That was—" Amy started.

"Terrible timing," William finished.

"The worst timing."

"Absolutely the worst."

They looked at each other, and then Amy started laughing. Not her cautious, professional laugh. The real one, the startled, surprised sound he'd been trying to coax out of her for days.

"We're never going to kiss, are we?" she said between laughs. "The universe is actively conspiring against us. First the alarm, now the janitor. Next time it'll be a fire alarm or a meteor strike."

"Next time we'll plan better."

"I thought we weren't planning."

"We'll plan to not be interrupted. That's allowed."

She continued laughing, and he realized he was laughing too, the tension easing into something more relaxed and simple.

"Are you hungry?" he asked as they walked out into the cold.

"Starving."

"There's a diner on Main Street. Not fancy, but the food's good and they're open late."

She pulled out her phone out of habit, he assumed, looked at her calendar, then put it away without checking anything.

"Sounds perfect," she said. "And I'm not even going to figure out how long we should stay or what this means for our professional working relationship."

"Look at you. Being spontaneous."

"Don't get used to it. This might be a temporary lapse in judgment."

"I'll take what I can get."

They walked together toward Main Street, and William tried not to think about how close they had been to kissing, how her eyes had looked in the lamplight, or how she had said his name right before the universe stepped in.

There would be another chance. There had to be. Because if the universe was conspiring against them this consistently, it meant what they were building mattered. And if it mattered, it was worth fighting for, even if that meant dealing with janitors who have terrible timing, phone alarms, and the constant threat of meteor strikes.

The dinner at the diner was a quiet success. They talked about the work they loved and the futures they imagined—different paths that, for this one night, ran side by side. But as the clock moved closer to midnight, a sudden, irresistible yawn pulled Amy back into the reality of exhaustion.

"I think the 412 stairs wore me out. I should head back to the Inn," she admitted.

"The Inn is a long, cold walk," William countered gently. "My apartment is right around the corner. I have a spare room with a lock on the door. You'll be safe."

She watched the snow, a thick, insistent curtain falling outside the steamy window. The long climb up the old windmill truly had sapped her strength. *Why not?* she thought, the idea suddenly feeling like the simplest, warmest path forward.

"Alright," she said, pulling her gaze away from the white storm. "If you don't mind. The bed at the Inn can wait."

They paid the bill, buttoned their coats, and left the warm, fluorescent glow of the diner for the quiet, snow-covered street. Amy followed William around the corner and headed down the block toward the side door of his building.

Chapter 9
Amy - December 12th

The woman in William's kitchen had a posture that resulted from years of practicing proper form.

Amy froze in the doorway, barefoot and undercaffeinated, watching this stranger reorganize William's spice rack with the confidence of someone who had done it before. The confidence of someone who belonged here.

William's back was to her, his shoulders tense in a way they hadn't been last night when he'd kissed her goodnight at the guest room door. When his hand had lingered on her waist just long enough to make her forget about spreadsheets entirely.

The woman turned, smiled, and extended a hand with nails the color of arterial bleeding.

"You must be Amy."

The voice was like warm honey poured over something sharp. Amy recognized the technique; she'd used it herself in a hundred corporate negotiations. The polite decimation.

"I am." Amy accepted the handshake, noticing the perfect manicure, the cashmere sweater that probably cost more than her monthly car payment, and the way this woman touched William's counter as if she were reconnecting with an old friend. "And you are?"

"Lila Northrop." The smile widened, showing teeth that had definitely benefited from professional whitening. "I'm sorry, I assumed William mentioned me. We were engaged."

Were. Past tense. Amy filed that away while her stomach did something complicated.

"He might have." Amy kept her voice level, friendly, utterly unconcerned. She was excellent at lying. "Coffee smells amazing."

"Doesn't it?" Lila lifted William's favorite mug, the chipped one from the historical society that he'd told Amy came from his grandfather's collection. "I brought it from that little roastery in Portland. The one William and I discovered on our trip to Maine. Remember, William? The place with the cranberry scones?"

William's jaw clenched. There it was, the tell. The small muscle that twitched when he was caught between competing disasters.

"That was a long time ago, Lila."

"Three years." Lila set down the mug carefully, exactly where Amy had been standing last night when William kissed her. "But some things you don't forget."

The kitchen was too warm, or maybe Amy was too warm. She should have changed out of yesterday's clothes and run a brush through her hair. She should have anticipated that spending the night at William's, in the guest room, fully clothed, after solving historical clues until midnight, would somehow lead to a morning surprise from a woman who looked like she'd stepped out of a Talbots catalog.

"I should get dressed," Amy said, already backing toward the hallway. "I didn't realize you had company."

Lila just stopped by to drop off some paperwork. William finally turned away from the coffee maker, his eyes meeting Amy's with what seemed like an apology, or maybe a plea. "For the historical society gala. She's on the planning committee."

"Co-chair, actually." Lila's smile stayed steady. "We're hoping William will give the keynote this year. He's so talented at making the past come alive."

The subtext was a flashing neon sign: *I know him. I know what he's good at. Do you?*

Amy's fingers grasped the doorframe so tightly that the wood grain left impressions on her palm. She wanted to run. She wanted to make a strategic retreat to the guest room, gather her things, and make a dignified exit before this conversation became any more unbearable.

But she'd spent two years building a career on not backing down. On facing uncomfortable situations with a smile and a plan.

So she smiled.

"That sounds wonderful," Amy said, casually moving into the kitchen. "William's been teaching me so much about Holly Falls history. Did you know the town founder proposed to his wife at the footbridge? William showed me the exact spot yesterday."

The temperature in the room shifted.

Lila's smile stayed perfectly steady, but a flicker of calculation passed behind her eyes. "How lovely. William does have a knack for romantic gestures. When he wants to make them."

The implication hit like a slap covered in velvet.

William placed his coffee mug down more forcefully than needed. "Lila."

"I'm just saying." Lila's voice remained light, conversational, yet sharp. "You were always so thoughtful about the big moments. It's the everyday things that tripped you up. The showing up. The staying."

Amy watched William's face close, observing as he retreated behind the careful neutrality he used when someone hit too close to a wound he wasn't ready to expose.

She recognized the look because she wore it herself, often.

"I should go." Lila collected her coat from the back of a chair, a chair Amy had sat in last night, laughing with William over his story about the town's eccentric founder. "I've clearly interrupted something. Amy, it was so nice to meet you. William's mentioned you a few times. I'm glad he's found someone to help with the Wish Box project."

Help. As if Amy was only that—a temporary assistant, a project manager for his nostalgia.

"The pleasure was mine," Amy said, her consultant voice smooth as glass. "And Lila? Those spices are alphabetized incorrectly. Cumin comes before curry powder."

Lila's smile froze. "Excuse me?"

"The spice rack." Amy pointed to the cabinet Lila had been reorganizing. "You've got curry before cumin. It's a common mistake."

For a brief, beautiful moment, Lila's composure faltered. Then she laughed, a tight, rehearsed sound. "Of course. How silly of me. William, I'll email you about the gala."

The door closed behind her with a gentle click that somehow sounded louder than a slam.

Silence filled the kitchen.

Amy poured herself coffee, added cream, and stirred exactly three times. The routine steadied her hands and gave her something to do besides look at William, who was staring at her with an expression she couldn't quite understand.

"So," Amy said finally, keeping her eyes on her coffee. "Ex-fiancée. That was exciting."

"I should have warned you."

"Warned me?" Amy looked up, surprised by the edge in her own voice. "Why would you warn me? We're just solving a mystery together. It's not like we're..." She trailed off, unsure how to finish that sentence.

Not dating. Not together. Not anything with a label or a timeline or a clear definition.

Just two people who had kissed under a lighthouse and solved historical riddles and somehow ended up in a situation where ex-fiancées felt entitled to show up at seven a.m. to reorganize spice racks.

"We're not just solving a mystery." William's voice was quiet but firm. "And you know it."

Amy's heart did something acrobatic. Inconvenient.

"Then what are we doing?"

He crossed the kitchen in three quick steps, stopping close enough that Amy could smell his soap, cedar and something darker. Close enough that she had to tilt her head back to meet his eyes.

"I don't know," he admitted. "But I'd like to find out if you're willing to stay long enough for me to figure it out."

Staying. Lila's word. The thing William apparently wasn't good at.

Amy thought about her apartment in New York. Her corner office that wasn't hers anymore. The careful, controlled life she had built that had somehow become a cage.

She reflected on yesterday, standing on the footbridge with William, listening to him share stories about the town founder's courtship. How the founder had been a meticulous man who kept detailed records of every decision except for the one to propose. That decision, he made on impulse—on a Tuesday afternoon in October. With no plan and no certainty except the feeling that this woman made him want to be reckless.

"I'm not good at reckless," Amy said. "I plan things. I prepare. I make spreadsheets."

"I know."

"I came to Holly Falls with a list. Seventeen names. Criteria. Color-coded risk assessments."

William's mouth twitched. "I remember."

"You weren't on the list."

"I know that too."

"But here I am," Amy said vaguely, gesturing towards the kitchen, herself in yesterday's clothes, and the situation that had somehow gone from a collision in the town square to her standing in William's kitchen, defending her choice to alphabetize his spices. "Barefoot in your kitchen. Lying to your ex-fiancée about how much you've taught me about local history."

"You weren't lying." William's hand found her elbow, his thumb tracing small circles on the inside of her arm. "I have been teaching you about local history."

"That's not the lie."

"What's the lie?"

Amy met his eyes. "That I'm here for the history."

The words hovered between them, sincere and terrifying.

William's hand moved from her elbow to her wrist, his fingers loosely circling. Anchoring without restraining. "Then why are you here?"

Because she'd kissed him at the lighthouse and forgot to be afraid. Because he made her laugh even during arguments. Because he looked at her as if she was fascinating instead of exhausting. Because for the first time in years, she wanted something she couldn't plan, optimize, or achieve through strategic execution.

She wanted him.

The realization sank into her chest, heavy, warm, and utterly terrifying.

"I'm here because you rearranged your entire afternoon yesterday to help me chase down a clue that might not even exist," Amy said finally. "Because you remembered I take my coffee with cream but no sugar. Because you didn't push when I wanted to stop at the guest room door last night even though we both knew that's not where I wanted to sleep."

William's eyes darkened. "Where did you want to sleep?"

"Don't make me say it."

"I'm going to need you to say it," his voice had gone rough. "Because I've spent the last three hours trying to convince myself that you're just here for the Wish Box. That you'll solve the clues and go back to New York and forget about Holly Falls and the cynical historian who can't seem to stop thinking about you."

"I don't want to go back to New York."

"Then stay."

"For how long?"

"How long do you want?"

Amy's laugh came out shaky. "That's not how I work. I need parameters. Timelines. Clear expectations."

"I can't give you those." William's thumb kept tracing circles on her wrist, slow and purposeful. "I can't promise a timeline or a plan. But I can promise this, if you stay, I'm all in. No spreadsheets. No risk assessments. Just us, figuring this out as we go."

The kitchen smelled like coffee, cedar, and the faint sweetness of cinnamon rolls someone had left on the counter, probably Lila's peace offering, now forgotten. Through the window, Amy saw snow beginning to fall, large flakes drifting down to cover the cobblestones in white.

Holly Falls looked like a snow globe. Perfect, contained, and completely separate from the real world where Amy was supposed to go back to her real life and her real problems.

Except this was beginning to feel more real than anything she'd left behind.

"Okay," Amy said.

"Okay?"

"Okay, I'll stay. I'll figure it out. I'll try not to alphabetize your entire life."

William grinned. "I make no promises about not enjoying it when you do."

He kissed her then, soft and slow, his hands gently holding her face as if she were something precious, something worth keeping.

Amy's carefully constructed defenses crumbled.

When they finally parted, William's forehead rested against hers, and they both took deep breaths.

"For the record," William murmured, "Lila left because I asked her to. Six months ago. She wanted me to move to Boston. Take a position at a bigger museum. Leave Holly Falls."

"And you said no."

"I said this is my home. My history. The place I'm supposed to protect." His hands slid down to her shoulders. "She said I was wasting my potential on a town that didn't matter."

Amy pulled back enough to meet his eyes. "She's wrong."

"I know." William smiled, but there was something sad in it. "She's also right. I could've had a bigger career. More prestige. But I would've been miserable. So I chose this."

"Do you regret it?"

"Not for a second." His hands tightened on her shoulders. "But she's not wrong about my track record with showing up. With staying. When things get difficult, my instinct is to retreat. To hide in the archives and pretend the present doesn't exist."

Amy recognized the confession for what it was, a warning. An honesty she hadn't expected.

"I retreat too," she admitted. "Into my lists. My plans. My conviction that if I just organize things correctly, I can avoid getting hurt."

"Has it worked?"

"Not even a little bit."

William laughed, the sound warm and genuine. "Then maybe we're both terrible at this."

"Spectacularly terrible."

"Want to be terrible together?"

Amy thought about the spreadsheet she'd deleted. The life she'd left behind. The certainty she'd traded for this messy, unplanned, utterly terrifying possibility.

"Yeah," she said. "I really do."

The snow was falling more heavily now, covering the world in white. Through the window, Amy could see townspeople starting their morning routines — the mail carrier making rounds, Mrs. Peterson walking her old poodle, the bakery owner shoveling snow from her front steps.

Holly Falls was waking up, and for the first time in years, Amy felt like she was waking up too.

"We should probably solve another clue today," William said, his arms still around her. "We're running out of time."

"We have fifteen days."

"Is that enough?"

Amy thought about the final clue, the one about surrender. About discovering truth within lies and finding reality in fantasy. About the key being hidden where one goddess walks and another waits.

She reflected on how each clue so far had demanded them to collaborate. To trust one another. To release control and accept uncertainty.

"It'll have to be," Amy said. "Because I'm not losing this. Not the quest. And not you."

William kissed her again, this time deeper, and Amy felt her last resistance melt away. She had come to Holly Falls with a plan: a list, a desperate need to prove she could find happiness on her own.

Instead, she'd found something better.

She'd found a reason to stop planning and start living.

Even if it terrified her.

Even if Lila's words about William's inability to stay echoed in the back of her mind like a warning she couldn't quite silence.

Even if the clock was ticking, the quest remained unsolved, and Kane was probably lurking somewhere, waiting for her to fail.

Right now, standing in William's kitchen with snow falling outside and coffee cooling on the counter, Amy let herself believe that maybe, just maybe, some things are worth the risk of not having a plan.

"So," William said, pulling back with a grin. "Footbridge? To look for the fourth clue?"

"Footbridge," Amy agreed. "But first, I need real clothes. And maybe breakfast that isn't just coffee and conversation."

"I can handle breakfast," William released her reluctantly, moving toward the refrigerator. "How do you feel about pancakes?"

"I feel like pancakes are an excellent decision."

"Good. Because they're the only thing I know how to make that doesn't come from a box."

Amy laughed, settling onto one of the kitchen stools. "This is going to be a disaster, isn't it?"

"Probably." William pulled out eggs, milk, and a box of pancake mix that definitely counted as "from a box" despite his claim. "But at least it'll be our disaster."

And somehow, that was the most romantic thing anyone had ever told her.

Chapter 10
William - December 14th

The lighthouse sat on the ridge overlooking Holly Falls, accessible by a winding trail that grew progressively steeper as it climbed. William had taken this hike dozens of times, as a kid with his grandfather, then as a teenager seeking solitude, and later as an adult maintaining the structure for the historical society.

He'd never made it with someone who gripped his hand tighter with every switchback.

"How much farther?" Amy asked, trying to sound casual and failing.

"Another quarter mile. Then four hundred and twelve steps to the observation deck."

"Four hundred and twelve."

"I've counted."

"Of course you have." She stumbled slightly on a root, and his hand shot out automatically to steady her. "Why did they build it so high?"

"Better visibility. The entire valley can be seen from the top. Ships used to navigate by it before the roads were built."

"Ships. In Vermont."

"Lake Champlain is forty miles that way. The lighthouse was part of a network." He kept his voice matter-of-fact, giving her something to focus on besides the increasing elevation. "Most of them are gone now. This is one of three still standing."

"And we have to climb all four hundred and twelve steps."

"We could stop at three hundred if you want. The clue won't be at the bottom, though."

"I hate you a little bit right now."

"No, you don't."

"No, I don't. But I'm considering it."

They reached the base of the lighthouse as the sun began sliding toward the horizon. The structure was made of stone, weathered but sturdy, with a wooden door that William unlocked using another key from his historical society collection.

Inside, the spiral staircase wound up into darkness. William pulled out a flashlight and offered Amy his free hand.

"You don't have to come up if heights bother you."

"Heights don't bother me. Falling from heights bothers me."

"The stairs are sturdy. My grandfather reinforced them in 1982. They're rated for twice our combined weight."

"You know the weight rating of stairs built in the 1880s."

"I know the weight rating of the reinforcements from 1982. The original stairs were questionable at best."

She looked up at the darkness above them. Took a breath. Put her hand in his.

"Four hundred and twelve steps."

"Give or take."

"I'm going to need you to be very specific about the 'give or take' part."

"Four hundred and twelve from bottom to top. I counted last month when I was up here cleaning the lamp mechanism."

They climbed together, with William leading and holding the flashlight, Amy's hand gripping his tightly. The stairs were narrow, barely wide enough for one person comfortably, so she stayed close behind him, close enough that he could hear her breathing and feel her presence like a physical weight.

At step one hundred, she said, "This is fine. This is totally fine."

At step two hundred, she said, "I take back every nice thing I've ever said about you."

At step three hundred, she stopped talking entirely and just concentrated on breathing.

At step four hundred, they reached the top.

The observation deck wrapped around the lighthouse's lamp room, enclosed by a waist-high iron railing that had been restored three years earlier. The space was small, about eight feet across, and the view was breathtaking.

Holly Falls sprawled below them, with the town square visible as a cluster of lights, the residential streets spreading out in neat grids, and the forest encircling everything like a protective wall. The sun hung low on the horizon, casting the sky in shades of orange, pink, and deep purple.

Amy grasped the railing, breathing heavily, and William stayed close enough to catch her if she lost her balance.

"Okay," she said after a moment. "This might be worth four hundred and twelve steps."

"Might be?"

"Is. Definitely is." She looked out at the valley, and something in her expression shifted. The fear gave way to wonder, and William found himself watching her instead of the view he'd seen a hundred times before.

The way the sunset caught in her hair. The way her eyes reflected the orange light. The way she smiled, not her careful professional smile, but something genuine and unguarded.

"It's beautiful," she said.

"It is."

She glanced at him, caught him watching her, and her cheeks flushed. "You're not even looking at the view."

"I'm looking at the best part."

"That's very smooth."

"That's very honest."

She turned back toward the valley, but she was smiling. "We should find the clue before we lose the light."

"Probably."

Neither of them moved.

Then Amy's organizational instincts kicked in, and she began a systematic search of the observation deck. William assisted by checking the areas he knew were most likely to contain carved text.

"Here." He found it carved into the main support beam at the top of the stairs, where the structure bore the weight of the lamp room. The text was small, protected from weather by the overhang, visible only if you knew to look up. "Final clue."

Amy pulled out her camera and took photos from multiple angles while William read aloud: "'Where all paths converge and wishes are born, where the key was hidden since the very first morn, return to the center, the start of the quest, where the answer awaits in the box you know best.'"

"The Wish Box," Amy said immediately. "The final clue is right on the box itself. It's in the town square where we began."

"We've been circling it the entire time."

"Looking everywhere except the obvious place," she laughed, the sound surprised and delighted. "I do that. Miss what's right in front of me because I'm too busy looking at the complicated solution."

"We both do that."

"We're very good at making things harder than they need to be."

"We're very good at protecting ourselves."

The words lingered between them, and Amy's smile dimmed slightly. "What are we protecting ourselves from?"

"From desiring something we might not receive. From hoping for something that may not succeed. From being brave enough to get hurt."

"That's very specific."

"That's very true." He moved closer, close enough that they were sharing space on the small deck, close enough that he could see the way her pupils had dilated. "Can I ask you something?"

"You're going to ask anyway."

"What do you truly want, Amy? Really want. Not what you think you should want, not what your spreadsheet says you should want. What do you really want?"

She remained silent for a long moment, her eyes fixed on the valley below. When she finally spoke, her voice was soft.

"I want to stop being afraid that if I'm not perfect, I'm not enough. I want to wake up and not immediately calculate how many things I need to accomplish to justify existing. I want to let people see the messy parts without believing they'll leave when they realize I'm work." She looked at him. "I want to stop organizing my way to happiness and just... be happy. Even if I don't deserve it."

"You deserve it."

"You don't know that."

"I recognize that you're smart, determined, and courageous enough to climb 412 stairs even when heights scare you. I see you turn off alarms to stay present. I understand you criticize ex-boyfriends who try to use you as a backup plan. I know you hold your sister's hand when she's afraid and record everything carefully because accuracy matters to you." He moved closer, within touching distance. And I know you believe you must earn love, but you don't. You are enough. You've always been enough."

Her eyes were shining. "William—"

"You're enough," he said again, pulling her close. "You're enough just as you are. Spreadsheets and color-coded calendars and all."

She was shaking. He could feel it as he held her, sense how her breath hitched, and see the tears beginning to form.

"Can I kiss you?" he asked.

She nodded, not trusting her voice.

He leaned down slowly, giving her time to change her mind, watching her eyes flutter shut. When his lips met hers, it was gentle at first, cautious, tentative, a question rather than a statement.

Then she made a small sound in the back of her throat, pressed closer, and careful became something entirely different.

Her hands reached up to his hair, fingers threading through it and pulling him down to her. His arms wrapped around her waist, lifting her slightly so she wouldn't have to stretch so far. She tasted like the coffee they had before the hike and something sweet she must have eaten while he wasn't looking.

The kiss grew more passionate. Her mouth responded beneath his, and he accepted the cue, exploring and discovering what caused her to gasp and tighten her grip on his hair.

Her back pressed against the lighthouse wall. He wasn't sure which of them moved first, and then she was caught between cold stone and his body, seemingly unbothered. Her hands moved from his hair to his shoulders, then down his chest, tracing him through his shirt, while his hands stayed firmly on her waist because moving them anywhere else felt like it might kill him.

"William—" She broke the kiss, breathing hard, her pupils blown wide.

"Too much?"

"Not enough." She pulled him back down, and this time there was nothing gentle about it.

His hands moved lower, cupping her hips and pulling her close against him. She made that sound again, the one that was destroying his self-control, and wrapped one leg around his, bringing them impossibly closer.

They were making out against a lighthouse wall like teenagers. They were visible to anyone with binoculars down in the valley. They should stop. They should definitely stop.

He pulled back just enough to press his forehead to hers, both of them breathing as if they'd climbed those 412 steps twice.

"We should—" he started.

"Don't say we should stop."

"I was going to say we should aim to avoid getting arrested for public indecency on a historical landmark."

She laughed, breathless and charming. "That would be bad for your historical society reputation."

"My reputation can handle it. You might have more concerns."

"My concerns are currently overruled by other priorities."

"Other priorities?"

"You." She kissed him again, softer this time. "This. Whatever this is that makes me forget why being careful is important."

When they finally separated, truly creating space between their bodies, Amy was crying.

"Hey." He wiped the tears away with his thumbs. "What's wrong? Did I—"

"Nothing's wrong." She laughed through her tears. "Everything's perfect. I'm perfect. I'm a mess. I'm terrified. I'm so okay."

"You're crying."

"I'm happy-crying. Is that a thing? Happy-crying?"

"I think so."

"Good. Because I'm doing it," she said as she wrapped her arms around his neck, holding on tight. "You make me feel things I didn't think I could feel. Things that don't fit into spreadsheets, calendars, or any kind of organizational system. And it's terrifying, but it's also the best thing that's happened to me in years."

He pulled her close again, simply holding her as the sun set and the stars began to appear above them. Holly Falls glowed below, Christmas lights twinkling like earthbound stars, and William felt something in his chest that could have been hope or certainty.

"I'm all in," he said. "If you are. I'm all in."

She pulled back just enough to look at him, her eyes still wet but smiling. "I'm in. I'm so in. I'm in despite the fact that it makes no logical sense, you're not on my list, and this whole thing is completely unplanned and a disaster waiting to happen."

"That's the most romantic thing anyone's ever said to me."

"I'm working on my romantic declarations. Give me time."

"Take all the time you need."

They stood there holding each other as the temperature dropped and the stars multiplied overhead, and William tried to memorize this moment. The way she fit against him. The way she smelled like citrus and something uniquely her. The way she looked at him like he was worth four hundred and twelve steps.

"We should go down," she said eventually. "Before we freeze to death."

"Probably."

"Or we could stay here and make out until hypothermia sets in."

"That's tempting."

"But impractical."

"Very impractical."

They descended together, hand in hand, pausing every fifty steps or so to kiss because neither of them could resist. By the time they reached the bottom, Amy was laughing, breathless, and looking at him as if he'd hung the stars himself.

"Tomorrow," William said as they walked back down the trail. "The Wish Box. We'll examine it together, find whatever's hidden there."

"And then what?"

"Then we've solved the mystery, finished the project, and fulfilled our obligation to Karen, the town, and the Christmas gala.

"And then?"

He stopped walking and turned to face her in the darkness. "And then we figure out what comes next. Together. Without the excuse of clues and riddles and historical projects."

"That sounds terrifying."

"It sounds perfect."

She kissed him again, right there on the trail with the lighthouse behind them and the town below them and the whole world narrowed down to this moment.

When they reached his truck, she pulled out her phone, opened the app where her spreadsheet was, and stared at it for a long moment.

"What are you doing?" he asked.

"Thinking about deleting it. The spreadsheet. The whole thing."

"Are you going to?"

"Soon. Maybe. Once I'm sure this is real and not just..." She trailed off.

"Not just what?"

"Not just me falling for someone who'll realize I'm too complicated and leave."

"Amy—"

"I know. I know you said I'm enough, and I'm trying to believe that. But the spreadsheet feels like insurance—like proof that if this doesn't work, I have other options."

He should have been hurt and felt insulted that she was keeping a backup plan while claiming to be all in.

Instead, he just felt tired. "Keep it as long as you need to. But know that I'm not planning on giving you a reason to need it."

"I know. I just… I need more time."

"Okay."

They drove back to the lodge in comfortable silence, and William walked her to the door because that was his thing now.

"Tonight was perfect," she said.

"It was."

"Tomorrow the Wish Box. And then—"

"And then we figure out the rest."

She kissed him goodnight, a genuine kiss, with her hands on his face and his on her waist, the kind that promised more kisses in the future.

William drove home feeling unstoppable, as if he'd scaled a lighthouse and kissed a woman who managed her fears with spreadsheets, somehow convincing her he was worth the risk.

He went to bed thinking about the way she'd said "I'm in," as if it were both a surrender and a victory.

He fell asleep believing the hard part was over.

He didn't realize that the spreadsheet she'd promised to delete was still there, backed up in three locations, ready to wipe out everything they'd just created.

He didn't know that in three days, he'd find it.

He didn't know that all the progress they'd made, all the vulnerability they'd shared, all the walls they'd torn down would come crashing back up in a single moment of betrayed trust.

He just knew that he was falling for Amy Donovan, and she was falling for him, and for tonight, that was enough.

Chapter 11
Amy - December 16th

Amy stared at her phone screen as if it had betrayed her.

PROJECT: CHRISTMAS HUSBAND – Final update

The notification banner glowed on her lock screen for three seconds. Three seconds during which William might have seen it. Might have read it. Might have interpreted it in the worst way.

She swiped it away like it burned, her heart hammering.

They sat at the Bean Counter, coffees steaming between them, and William's smile no longer quite reached his eyes. Too casual. Too cautious. Like he was weighing a decision.

"Coffee?" His voice had that particular neutrality which meant he was thinking too hard.

"Sure." Her voice came out thinner than usual.

She woke up happy this morning. Truly happy. Not the stressed, checklist-finished type, but the silly, ceiling-grinning, lovestruck-teen kind. The kind she hadn't experienced since she was young enough to believe happiness didn't need a five-year plan.

William had texted her at seven: *Coffee before we tackle the final clue? I have theories.*

She'd responded at once: *Your theories or actual solutions?*

Both. Neither. Come find out.

She'd laughed out loud while brushing her teeth, catching her own reflection grinning at nothing and not feeling embarrassed about it.

That had been thirty minutes ago.

Now they sat with untouched drinks, and Amy could still feel the phantom echo of that notification burning against her palm.

"Everything okay?" William asked.

"Fine. Just, work email. Nothing important." The lie tasted bitter. She took a sip of coffee to wash it away. The liquid was too hot, burned her tongue, and added physical discomfort to the churning in her stomach.

He watched her for a moment longer, then seemed to decide to let it go. "Ready to look at the Wish Box again?"

"Always."

They walked to the town square, and Amy tried to recapture the happiness from an hour ago. She focused on William's hand almost-but-not-quite brushing hers as they strolled. On the way, the December sunlight caught the Christmas decorations and made everything look like a snow globe coming to life.

But the notification kept echoing in her mind. *Final update.* What did that even mean? She'd set several reminders weeks ago, back when the spreadsheet still felt like insurance instead of evidence.

The Wish Box sat in its usual spot, ornate, locked, and legendary. William moved around it slowly, running his fingers along the brass edges, while Amy watched how his hands moved—careful, reverent, like he was reading braille.

"There," he said suddenly. "I knew I'd seen something here before but couldn't quite make it out."

He knelt, traced something with his fingertip. Amy knelt beside him, close enough to smell his coffee-and-old-books scent, close enough to feel his warmth in the December cold.

The brass felt icy beneath her fingers, rough from age and weather. She could sense the faint grooves of engraved letters, nearly smooth from time and touch.

"What does it say?" she whispered.

William leaned closer, his shoulder pressed against hers. "'The key is not to seek but to surrender.'"

Amy's stomach dropped. "That's it? That's the final clue?"

"Apparently."

She sat back on her heels, frustration growing. The town square around them hummed with late-morning activity, cars passing on Main Street, the bell above the bakery door chiming as customers entered, children's voices from the park. All of it felt distant and unimportant compared to the locked box and its maddening secret.

"That's not a clue. That's a fortune cookie."

"It's a philosophical instruction."

"It's useless." She stood, brushed off her knees with more force than necessary. "How am I supposed to tell the entire town, the town that's counting on us and sold out the gala based on our promise to solve this, that the answer is to stop looking and surrender? We'll tell them if they feel worthy enough, the box might pop open on vibes? That should impress the press."

"Amy—"

"No, seriously. The Mayor is expecting a solution. My parents are coming to the gala. Dawn is watching me try to prove I can do something without over-planning it. And the answer is 'be vulnerable and magic happens'?" She could hear her voice rising, feel the familiar panic of a project spiraling beyond her control. "That's not a solution. That's giving up."

William stood, brushed the dirt from his jeans. His face was carefully neutral again. The same too-casual expression from the coffee shop. "Maybe that's the point."

"What point?"

"Maybe the Wish Box doesn't open because you solve riddles or find hidden keys. Maybe it opens when you stop trying to control the outcome."

The words landed like a challenge. Like an accusation.

Amy felt her jaw tighten. "So you're saying I'm the problem. My need for control is why we can't solve this."

"That's not what I said."

"It's what you meant," she said, crossing her arms, feeling defensive and hating that she's being defensive. "I'm trying to help. I'm trying to make sure we deliver on what we promised the town. If that makes me controlling, then fine. But at least I'm not suggesting we hope really hard and see what happens."

"Amy." His voice was gentle, which somehow made it worse. "I'm not criticizing you. I'm trying to understand the clue."

"The clue is telling me to be someone I'm not."

Or it's suggesting that pretending to be someone you're not may be what's holding you back from what you want.

The silence that followed was sharp enough to cut.

Amy felt tears prick her eyes and blinked them back furiously. This was ridiculous. They were arguing over a metaphorical instruction engraved on a legendary box that, in reality, didn't have a visible opening mechanism. This wasn't worth getting upset about.

Except it was. Because William wasn't only talking about the Wish Box.

"I need to go," she said abruptly. "I have… I need to check on something for the gala."

"Amy, wait—"

"I'll see you at the planning meeting this afternoon. Two PM. Community center." She was already backing away, putting distance between them. "We can figure out what to tell the Mayor then."

She walked away before he could answer, before she could see if his too-casual expression had changed into something else. Before she could fully realize that she'd run from him because a metaphorical clue had felt too much like a mirror.

Her phone buzzed in her pocket. She pulled it out, half-hoping it was William sending an apology, explanation, or something to make this less terrible.

It wasn't.

It was another notification from the spreadsheet app: *Reminder: Review backup files.*

Amy looked at it, at the evidence that a part of her was still protecting herself with insurance policies against heartbreak, and felt something in her chest break.

She opened the app. Stared at the file labeled *PROJECT_CHRISTMAS_HUSBAND_BACKUP.xlsx* that she'd forgotten existed until this moment.

She should delete it. Should have deleted it weeks ago, the moment William told her she didn't have to earn this.

Instead, she closed the app and shoved her phone back in her pocket.

Later. She'd deal with it later.

Right now, she needed to focus on the gala planning meeting. On concrete tasks with measurable outcomes. On things she could control.

The community center was chaotic when Amy arrived at 1:45.

Volunteers everywhere, all of them with questions. The caterer needed menu approval. The sound system wasn't working. Someone had ordered the wrong color tablecloths and now there was a dispute about whether cream was close enough to ivory.

Amy dove into it with relief. This was familiar territory. Problems with solutions. Crises that could be managed with organization and follow-through.

She pulled out her tablet, began a task list, assigned responsibilities, and created a timeline. Within twenty minutes, half the problems were solved, and the remaining issues had clear paths to resolution.

Mayor Karen appeared at her side. "Amy, thank goodness. You're a miracle worker."

"Just organization."

"Still miraculous." Karen lowered her voice. "Have you and William figured out the final clue?"

Amy's stomach clenched. "We're working on it."

"I know the presentation is in a week, but the press is already asking questions. They want to know if we've solved it or if this is a publicity stunt." Karen's smile was strained. "I told them of course we've solved it. We have solved it, haven't we?"

"We have the clue. We're just, interpreting it."

"Interpreting it." Karen's smile stayed steady, but her eyes became sharper. "That sounds concerning."

"It's metaphorical. The final instruction. It requires some thought."

"Thought is good. Thought is fine," Karen patted her arm. "Just make sure the thought turns into something concrete by the twenty-fourth. The town is counting on you both."

She hurried away, and Amy stood there feeling the weight of those expectations settling on her shoulders like snow.

The town was counting on them. The press was watching. Her parents would be in the audience. Dawn would be there with Jack and Lily, watching Amy try to prove she could do something without her usual safety nets.

And the answer was *surrender.*

Her phone buzzed. Text from William: *I'm sorry about earlier. Can we talk before the meeting?*

Amy typed: Already at the community center. Meeting in 10 minutes.

His response came right away: *After the meeting then?*

She looked at the message, at the olive branch he was offering, and felt the crack in her chest widen just a bit.

She typed: *Maybe. We'll see.*

Not a yes. Not a no. Just cautious distance while she figured out how to feel about a man who saw through her walls and a clue that demanded she tear them down.

William arrived precisely at two PM, which meant he'd likely been outside for five minutes, waiting to avoid being early or late. The thought made her smile despite everything.

He caught her eye across the room, and something in his face softened. Not quite an apology, not quite forgiveness for whatever had happened that morning, but an acknowledgment that they were both trying.

The meeting began. Amy took notes, created action items, and assigned tasks. William provided historical context for the decorations, answered questions about the Wish Box legend, and charmed the volunteers with stories about past gala celebrations.

They worked well together, even now, despite the morning's argument lingering between them.

Mrs. Peterson cornered them afterward. "You two make such a lovely team. The whole town is so excited about your presentation."

"Thank you," Amy said automatically.

"Have you figured out the last clue? I keep trying to remember what opened the box twenty-five years ago, but I was out of town that Christmas and missed the whole thing."

William and Amy exchanged a glance.

"We're close," William said.

"That's wonderful! I just knew you two would figure it out. You're perfect together." Mrs. Peterson beamed at them like a proud grandmother. "Don't let her go, William. Girls like Amy don't come around every day."

She walked away, and Amy felt her cheeks heat.

"Sorry about that," William said quietly. "Mrs. Peterson has been trying to matchmake since I moved back to town."

"It's fine. She means well."

They stood there in awkward silence, surrounded by departing volunteers and the lingering tension from this morning.

"Amy," William started. "About what I said earlier—"

"It's fine. You were interpreting the clue."

"I wasn't trying to criticize you."

"I know." She did know. Intellectually. But her defensive instincts had kicked in anyway, protecting her from the vulnerability the clue demanded. "I just... I don't know how to not have a plan. I don't know how to approach something this important and surrender to uncertainty."

"I know. That's what makes you good at what you do."

"But it's also what's preventing me from solving this." She looked at the tablet in her hands, at the perfectly organized task list. "The clue is telling me to be someone I'm not. And I don't know if I can do that."

"Maybe it's not about becoming someone else. Maybe it's about giving yourself permission to be yourself without the armor."

The words settled between them, gentle and devastating.

"I should go," Amy said. "I have seventeen follow-up tasks from this meeting, and I need to—"

"Amy." He caught her hand. "Can we try again? Tomorrow? Coffee and conversation, no clues or arguments or pressure?"

She looked at his hand holding hers, at how his thumb brushed her knuckles without him seeming to notice.

"Maybe," she said. "I'll let you know."

She softly pulled away, grabbed her things, and left before he saw that her eyes were watering again.

Outside, the December air was crisp and cold. Christmas lights had already begun to glow in the early twilight. The town looked perfect, charming, and cozy, just like the kind of place where wishes come true.

Amy grabbed her phone, looked at the spreadsheet app, and decided.

She opened the backup file and looked at the list of seventeen names, focusing on William's entry in slot number four, along with all the careful notes she'd made about compatibility, risk assessment, and decision points.

Her finger hovered over the delete button.

She should delete it right now to prove to herself that she is brave enough to surrender the safety net.

Instead, she closed the app and walked back to the lodge.

Tomorrow. She'd deal with it tomorrow.

Tonight, she had to face the uncomfortable truth that the Wish Box had given her the answer weeks ago, and she'd been too afraid to listen.

The key is not to seek but to surrender.

She had been searching since her arrival in Holly Falls. Searching for control, for certainty, and for proof that she could shape her path to happiness.

Maybe it was time to stop seeking.

Maybe it was time to fall.

Chapter 12
William - December 17th

William hadn't slept.

He'd tried. Gone through all the motions, changed into pajamas, brushed his teeth, and climbed into bed. He laid there, staring at the ceiling while his mind replayed the same three seconds on an endless loop.

Amy's phone screen lighting up.

The notification banner appearing.

PROJECT: CHRISTMAS HUSBAND - Final update

Three seconds. That's all it had been. Three seconds that had demolished every piece of progress they'd made.

He'd been standing behind her, close enough to see the screen over her shoulder. Close enough to read the words before she'd dismissed the notification with the speed of someone who desperately didn't want it seen.

He'd tried to rationalize it. Maybe it was a joke. Maybe it was work-related, she was a consultant, maybe she used that terminology for client projects. Maybe "Christmas Husband" was some kind of code name for something completely innocent.

Except her face when she'd dismissed it. The flash of panic. The way she'd immediately pulled up a different app, like she could make him forget what he'd seen.

And the word "final." Final update. As if she was wrapping up a project, completing an assignment, or finishing what she'd started.

He got out of bed at 5 AM, gave up on sleep, and went down to the shop. Turned on the lights. Made coffee. Tried to focus on cataloging the boxes of documents he'd been avoiding.

Instead, he was at his computer, typing "Amy Donovan consulting" into the search bar.

Her firm's website appeared first. Professional, sleek, exactly what he'd expected.

Strategic Life Planning Services

We help clients optimize their personal and professional trajectories through data-driven analysis and systematic implementation.

He clicked on her bio page.

Amy Donovan, Senior Consultant - Personal Life Planning

Specializing in relationship optimization, family planning strategies, and long-term goal execution, Amy adopts a methodical approach to life's most crucial decisions. She assists clients in creating actionable plans to achieve their personal objectives.

His stomach dropped.

Relationship optimization. Strategic planning. Data-driven analysis.

Was that what he was? A data point in her relationship optimization strategy?

He closed the laptop, pressed his hands against his eyes, and tried to think clearly.

She had told him she came to Holly Falls with a plan. She admitted to having a spreadsheet with seventeen candidates. She said she was falling for him, and that the plan no longer made sense.

But she also said she wasn't deleting the spreadsheet, because she needed it as insurance and wanted to know she had options.

And now there was a notification. A final update. On a project called CHRISTMAS HUSBAND.

The shop door swung open. William looked up to see Jack standing there with two coffees and the look of someone who'd been called by best friend telepathy.

"You look like hell," Jack said, handing him one of the coffees.

"Didn't sleep."

"Figured. Dawn texted me at midnight, saying Amy was freaking out about you being distant and not answering your phone. I'm here for emotional support or tough love, whichever you need."

"I saw something on Amy's phone yesterday."

"What kind of something?"

"A notification from a spreadsheet app. It said 'PROJECT: CHRISTMAS HUSBAND - Final update.'"

Jack's eyebrows rose. "Oh."

"Yeah."

"Did you ask her about it?"

"No. She dismissed it so fast, I don't think she knows I saw."

"So ask her now. This morning. Before you spiral into worst-case scenarios."

"What if she lies?"

"What if she doesn't?"

"What if it's true, Jack?" William set down his coffee and turned to face his friend. "What if I'm just another project? Another candidate in her systematic approach to finding a husband before Christmas?"

"That's not what I've seen when you're together."

"What have you seen?"

"I've seen her look at you as if you hung the moon. I've seen her turn off alarms, close spreadsheets, and climb four hundred steps despite being terrified of heights. I've seen her hold your hand in public even though everyone was watching. That's not someone treating you like a project."

"But she has a project. Literally. Called CHRISTMAS HUSBAND."

"So ask her about it. Directly. Give her a chance to explain."

"What if the explanation is worse than what I'm imagining?"

"What if it's better?" Jack leaned against the counter and crossed his arms. "Look, I get it. Ava burned you, making you feel like a character in her story instead of a real person. But Amy's not Ava. Amy's scared and controlling, and she probably has seventeen backup plans for every conversation, but she's not fake. She's just terrified."

"Of what?"

"Of being exactly what you're accusing her of. Of being too much work, too complicated, too broken to be worth the effort." Jack's voice softened. "Sound familiar?"

It did. That was the problem. He understood Amy's fear because he felt it too—the fear that maybe he wasn't enough, that maybe the person he'd fallen for would realize he was more trouble than he was worth.

But understanding her fear didn't make the spreadsheet disappear.

"I need to talk to her," William said.

"Yes, you do."

"What if she confirms everything I'm afraid of?"

"Then you'll know. And you can decide what to do with that information. But right now you're making decisions based on a three-second glimpse of a notification. That's not fair to either of you."

William pulled out his phone and typed a message: Can you meet me at the café in an hour? We need to talk.

Her response came almost immediately: *Of course. See you there.*

The hour dragged on. William attempted to work, tried to concentrate on anything other than the upcoming conversation. He failed spectacularly.

At 9:58, he walked to the café, found a table in the corner away from the main crowd but still visible enough that Mrs. Peterson and her gossip circle would definitely notice.

Amy arrived precisely at 10:00, as always on time. She was wearing jeans and a sweater, with her hair pulled back. When she saw him, her face brightened with a smile that made his chest ache.

She reached for his hand as she sat down.

He pulled back.

Her smile faltered. "Hi?"

"Hi." His voice sounded colder than he'd meant. He tried to soften it, but failed. "Thanks for meeting me."

Sure. Is everything all right? You seemed off yesterday, and then your text this morning sounded—" She paused. "What's wrong?

He should ease into this. He should ask gentle leading questions. He should give her the benefit of the doubt.

Instead, he heard himself say, "Do you have a plan for this? For us?"

She froze. "What?"

173

"A plan. A strategy. A systematic approach to our relationship."

"I don't... where is this coming from?"

"Just answer the question, Amy. Do you have a plan for us?"

Her eyes widened, and a look of panic flickered across her face. "I don't know what you mean."

"I think you do."

"William, what is this about?"

"PROJECT: CHRISTMAS HUSBAND." He said it quietly, watching her face. "I saw it on your phone yesterday. The notification. 'Final update.'"

All the color drained from her face. "That's... it's not—"

"Not what?"

"It's nothing. Just a silly thing I made before I met you. It doesn't mean anything."

"So I'm on it? This spreadsheet project is about finding a Christmas husband?"

She hesitated.

It was barely a second. Maybe half a second. But it was there, clear as day, and it told him everything he needed to know.

"It doesn't matter now," she said finally. "That was from before. Before we were—"

"It matters to me." He leaned back, creating some distance between them. "Was I candidate number what? Four? Five?"

"William—"

"Did you have compatibility metrics, success probabilities, or a timeline for relationship milestones?"

"Stop."

"Am I being optimized, Amy? Is this relationship part of your strategic life planning?"

"You're being cruel."

"I'm being honest, which is more than I can say for you right now."

She reached for him across the table. He stood, putting real distance between them, and her hand dropped back to the table.

"I need to think," he said. "I need space to figure out if anything we've done together was real or if I've just been checking boxes on your list."

"It's real. All of it. The spreadsheet was just, it was fear, it was insurance, it was me being stupid and desperate—"

"It was you treating me like a project." He grabbed his coat. "I'll see you at the next planning meeting. We still have to present at the gala. Professionally."

"William, please."

"I need to think, Amy."

He left before she could say anything more, leaving her sitting alone at the table while the entire café watched. He left because staying felt like accepting that being someone's candidate number four was okay.

Outside, the December air hit him like a slap. He wandered aimlessly, just moving, trying to burn off the anger, hurt, and betrayal churning inside his chest.

His phone buzzed. Text from Jack: *How'd it go?*

William typed back: *She didn't deny it. She just said it didn't matter.*

Did you let her explain?

She tried to laugh it off. Said it was silly. But when I asked if I was on it, she hesitated.

Maybe she was just scared.

Or maybe she was trying to decide how much truth to tell.

He shoved the phone into his pocket and kept walking.

The worst part wasn't the spreadsheet itself. It was that she'd kept it. That even after everything, the chapel, the lighthouse, the dinner with Jack, the kiss that had felt like coming home, she'd kept it and maintained it. Set reminders to update it.

Final update. Like she was finishing an assignment.

His phone buzzed again. He ignored it.

By the time he returned to the shop, he had six texts from Amy, each more desperate than the last.

Please let me explain

I know how it appeared, but it's not what you think.

The spreadsheet was from before. I haven't touched it since the chapel

I was going to delete it, I was just scared

William please

I love you

That last one stopped him cold.

She'd never said that before. Not directly. Not clearly.

And now she was saying it in a text message, as damage control, after he'd caught her treating their relationship like a project.

He didn't respond.

The day blurred by with not working, not thinking, and definitely not checking his phone every five minutes to see if she'd texted again.

By evening, he'd convinced himself he was overreacting. That he should call her, let her explain properly, and give her the benefit of the doubt Jack kept insisting she deserved.

Then he remembered her face when he'd asked if he was on the spreadsheet. That hesitation. That fraction of a second where she'd decided how much truth to tell.

His phone rang. Jack.

"Are you wallowing?" Jack asked without preamble.

"I'm processing."

"You're wallowing. Dawn says Amy's been crying all afternoon. Says she's trying to figure out how to explain without making it worse."

"There's no explanation that makes it better."

"Maybe not. Or maybe you're so convinced you're not worth someone's genuine effort that you're sabotaging the first real thing you've had in three years."

"That's not fair."

"None of this is fair. She shouldn't have kept the spreadsheet. You shouldn't have walked out without letting her explain. You're both scared people doing scared people things."

"I saw her professional bio, Jack. 'Relationship optimization.' 'Strategic life planning.' That's literally her job. And I'm apparently one of her projects."

"Or maybe she uses work terminology for everything because that's how her brain functions. Maybe she made a spreadsheet because organization makes her feel secure. Maybe she's just as scared of losing you as you are of being used."

"She hesitated when I asked if I was on it."

"Because she was scared, you idiot. Because you were looking at her like she'd betrayed you, and she knew anything she said would confirm what you already believed."

William was quiet for a long moment. "What if she really did see me as just another candidate? What if all of this, the vulnerability, the connection, the kiss on the lighthouse, what if it was all part of her systematic approach to achieving her objective?"

"Do you really believe that?"

"I don't know what I believe anymore."

Then talk to her. Actually speak to her. Let her explain without walking out. Give her a genuine chance.

"What if the explanation is worse than what I'm imagining?"

"What if it's not?"

After Jack hung up, William sat in his shop surrounded by history and tried to figure out what he truly wanted.

He wished Amy had never created the spreadsheet. He wanted to forget that she approached finding a husband with the same method she used for client projects. He wished the last two weeks had been spontaneous, genuine, and unplanned.

But they weren't. She had come to Holly Falls with a plan. She'd had numerous candidates. He didn't even know his number.

And yet.

And yet, when she kissed him on the lighthouse, she was crying from both joy and fear. When she admitted she was falling for him, her hands shook. When she climbed those four hundred and twelve steps despite her terror, she did it because he asked.

Maybe Jack was right. Perhaps he was sabotaging this because intentionally being hurt felt safer than accidentally being hurt.

His phone buzzed. It was a text from an unknown number.

He opened it to find a photo on Amy's phone screen, the full notification he'd seen yesterday, along with a screenshot of the spreadsheet itself.

The message below read: *She thought you should see the whole thing. So you understand what you're actually dealing with. -Dawn*

William opened the attachment, his stomach knotting.

The spreadsheet was there in full detail. Seventeen names. Compatibility percentages. Risk assessments. Timeline recommendations.

And there, in slot number four: *William Crane, 32, Historian/Business Owner*

Below his name: pages of notes. Observations. Assessments.

Strengths: Local ties, intelligent, skilled with hands (verified through observation), unexpectedly handsome, owns a successful business, genuine passion for work.

Weaknesses: Excessive cynicism, resistance to planning, appears commitment-averse, irritating know-it-all tendencies

Compatibility Probability: 63% → 58% → 71% → DELETED - no longer relevant

Status: OBSTACLE → ASSET → NOT A CANDIDATE. This is real. Stop treating it like a project.

Notes: Makes me laugh. Really laugh. Makes me want to throw the entire plan away. Makes me believe I might deserve something real. DELETE THIS SPREADSHEET.

The last entry was dated December 10th. The day they'd kissed on the lighthouse.

Below it, in a separate note: *Final update (scheduled 12/16): Decision made. Keeping William. Deleting everything else. This was never about finding a husband. It was about finding him.*

William stared at the screen for a long time.

She deleted his probability ratings, changed his status from CANDIDATE to NOT A CANDIDATE, and wrote notes to herself about how he made her feel.

And she'd scheduled a final update to document that she was choosing him, that she was no longer treating their relationship like a project.

The notification he'd seen, PROJECT: CHRISTMAS HUSBAND - Final update, wasn't about maintaining the spreadsheet.

It had been about closing it.

"Fuck," he said to the empty shop.

He'd walked out on her, refusing to let her explain. He accused her of treating him like a project, even though she'd been trying to delete the project entirely.

He took his keys, put on his coat, and went to the door.

He'd been an idiot. A scared, self-sabotaging idiot who'd proven every fear she'd ever had about not being enough.

He needed to fix this now, before she decided he's just like Peter, someone who'd leave when she showed him the complicated parts.

His phone rang. Amy.

He answered. "I'm sorry."

"Don't." Her voice was thick with tears. "Don't apologize. You were right. I should have deleted it weeks ago. I should have told you about it. I should have—"

"I saw the whole thing. Dawn sent me screenshots. Amy, I'm sorry. I didn't let you explain. I just assumed—"

"You assumed exactly what the evidence suggested, that I was treating you like a project." She laughed, but it sounded broken. "And I was, at first. But then you became something else. Something I didn't know how to categorize or control or plan for. And instead of telling you that, I just kept the spreadsheet as insurance because I was terrified of needing you."

There was a long silence. She could hear him breathing and almost feel him thinking on the other end of the line.

"Where are you?" he asked finally.

"The lodge. In my room. Crying and eating ice cream and wishing I'd never made the stupid spreadsheet in the first place."

"Amy." He paused briefly before resuming. "We need to have an honest conversation. Face to face. But you're upset, and I'm... I'm still hurt and confused, and I don't think either of us is in the right headspace for that right now."

"So what do we do?"

"We'll talk tomorrow when we're both calmer, when we can actually listen to each other instead of just reacting," he paused. "Can you do that? Can you wait until tomorrow?"

She wanted to say no. She also wanted to beg him to come over right now, fix this immediately, and not leave her alone with this terrible uncertainty for another night.

But he was right. She was crying too hard to be coherent. He was too hurt to be fair. They'd just make it worse.

"Okay," she managed. "Tomorrow. Where?"

I'll message you in the morning. We'll find a quiet spot, somewhere we can actually talk.

"William—" She didn't know what she wanted to say. Saying "I love you" felt like too much. Saying "I'm sorry" felt like too little. "Thank you. For not just giving up on me."

"I'm not giving up," his voice was quiet. "I'm just trying to figure out how to do this without hurting both of us more."

"Okay."

"Try to get some sleep."

"You too."

He hung up, and Amy sat in her room holding her phone, with ice cream melting beside her, trying to believe that tomorrow would be better.

It had to be better.

It couldn't get much worse.

Chapter 13
Amy - December 19th

Amy had been trying to catch William alone for two days.

Two days of arriving at the Bean Counter knowing he'd be there, only to find him already gone. Two days of walking past his shop during hours he was usually working, only to see the CLOSED sign. Two days of texting him to meet, getting responses like "Busy with inventory," "Historical society meeting," or "Rain check?"

He was avoiding her.

She had caused him to start avoiding her.

The panic that had been growing since the café confrontation was now spiraling out of control. Everything was crumbling. This was precisely what she had always feared: being too much trouble, too complicated, too inherently broken, and that the person she cared about would see it and walk away.

Except William hadn't left yet. He was just... creating distance. Which somehow felt worse.

Old instincts kicked in. She knew she could fix this. All she needed was a plan. A strategy. The right words in the right order, delivered at the right moment.

She opened her laptop and started writing.

Dear William,

I need to explain about the spreadsheet. I know how it looked, and I know you're hurt, but please let me—

She stopped. Read it back. It sounded defensive. Like she was making excuses.

She deleted it. Started again.

William,

I'm sorry. I'm so sorry. I should have told you about the spreadsheet from the beginning. I should have deleted it the moment I realized I was falling for you. I should have—

She blinked back tears. This wasn't an apology, it was a plea. And it sounded like begging.

Delete. Try again.

I made the spreadsheet because I was terrified. Because I'm twenty-nine and I've never had a relationship that didn't end with me being told I'm too much work. Because I thought that if I could just approach finding a husband strategically, I could control the outcome. I could guarantee I wouldn't end up alone.

But then I met you, and—

She stopped. Too much about her fear, not enough about him. He'd think this was still all about her.

Delete.

By the eighth draft, her laptop was covered in tears she hadn't realized she was crying, and every version sounded wrong. Too emotional. Too cold. Too defensive. Too desperate. Too focused on her wound. Not focused enough on his hurt.

She couldn't fix this with words on paper.

She needed to speak with him directly. Face to face. Let him see she was serious about every word.

Except he wouldn't meet with her face-to-face.

Her phone rang. Dawn.

"Can you come to my room?" Dawn's voice was thick with tears. "I need... I just need you."

Amy found her sister curled up on the bed, mascara smeared down her face, looking devastated.

"What happened?"

"Jack asked me to spend Christmas with his family. Real Christmas. Not just dinner, but Christmas morning with presents, Lily, his parents, and everyone. He asked me to be there. To be part of it."

"That's good, isn't it? That's what you wanted."

"That's terrifying. That's commitment. That's him asking me to be part of his family." Dawn's voice rose. "So I panicked and told him I'm leaving on the 26th, as I planned that this was always temporary. That I never promised to stay."

"Oh, Dawn."

"And he got so quiet. That scary quiet where you know someone is furious but trying not to yell. And then Lily came running in asking why we were talking angry, and I tried to explain but she just started crying, and Jack picked her up and looked at me like I was a monster who'd just broken his daughter's heart, and—" She dissolved into sobs.

Amy climbed onto the bed, wrapping her arms around her sister. "You're not a monster. You're just scared."

"I made a five-year-old to cry because I was too scared to stay."

"You made a five-year-old cry because you're trying to protect yourself. It's not the same thing."

"Isn't it?" Dawn pulled back and wiped her face. "We're doing the same thing, aren't we? Running from the people who truly want us because staying feels too dangerous."

"I'm not running. I'm trying to fix—"

"You're trying to control, which is just running in circles with extra steps." Dawn's voice was gentle but firm. "You made a spreadsheet to manage your fear of being alone. I kept my apartment lease in Portland to manage mine. We're both so scared of being hurt that we're just ensuring it happens."

"So what do we do?"

"We stop."

"How?"

"I don't know." Dawn laughed, but it sounded broken. "I really don't know. How can you stop running when running is the only thing that's ever kept you safe?"

They sat together, two sisters who had learned to shield themselves in different ways, both recognizing that their defenses had become a prison.

"I need to talk to William," Amy finally said, "actually talk to him. Let him see the whole spreadsheet, explain why I made it, why I kept it, and why I was too scared to delete it even after I knew I was falling for him."

"Will he listen?"

"I don't know. But I have to try."

She walked to William's shop before she lost her courage. It was almost six, closing time. She could see him through the window, turning off lights and organizing his workspace with his usual methodical care.

When she reached the door, he was locking it from the inside.

She knocked. "William. Please. I know you don't want to talk to me, but I need five minutes. Just five minutes to explain."

He looked at her through the glass for a long moment. She watched him debate, almost walk away, and finally unlock the door.

"Fine." His voice was tired. Flat. "Explain."

She stepped inside. He didn't back away from the door or invite her further in. Just stood there with his arms crossed, waiting.

"The spreadsheet, PROJECT: CHRISTMAS HUSBAND, I made it before I came here. I was desperate and scared, and I thought if I could just approach finding a husband like a work project, I could control the outcome. I could make sure I didn't end up alone."

"I already know all this. You told me at the café."

"I understand, but I need you to see why. I need you to realize it wasn't about you. It was about me being scared that I'm unlovable unless I'm perfect."

"Am I on the spreadsheet, Amy? Yes or no."

"Yes."

"What did it say about me?"

She tried to remember. Tried to recall the exact words she'd written weeks ago before deleting them. "It said, you were smart. And passionate about your work. And good with your hands, I'd seen you fix a shelf. And you had local ties, which was important for the long-term plan."

"I was a line item."

"You were a person I was trying to categorize because categories feel safe, and you made me feel anything but safe."

"What else did it say?"

"I don't remember exactly. I deleted most of it after the chapel. After you—" She stopped, her throat tightening. "After you told me I didn't have to earn this."

"Most of it. Not all of it."

"I was going to delete the rest. The final update notification, that wasn't about maintaining the project. That was supposed to be me documenting that I was choosing you. That I was done treating this like a project."

"Supposed to be?"

"I never got to make the update. You saw the notification before I could—" She stopped, seeing his expression. "You don't believe me."

"I don't know what to think. You're a consultant who specializes in strategic life planning. Making plans for people is literally your job. And I'm apparently one of your projects."

"You're not a project."

"Then what am I?" He stepped closer, and she saw the hurt beneath the anger. "Did you choose me because I met your criteria? Or did you choose me despite them?"

The question hung between them, sharp and devastating.

She wanted to say "despite them." She wanted to say she'd chosen him because he made her laugh, feel safe, and believe she could be messy without being abandoned. She wanted to say the criteria had stopped mattering the moment he'd caught her in a basement and told her that history lived in the small details.

But she couldn't bring herself to say it. Because the truth was more complicated than that.

She noticed him because he met the criteria. She paid attention because he checked the boxes. She gave him a chance because her spreadsheet indicated he was worth exploring.

And then she really fell for him. Messily, fully, and honestly fell for him.

But she couldn't distinguish the beginning from the middle. She couldn't claim she'd chosen him purely despite the criteria when the criteria explained why she'd noticed him at all.

"I don't know," she said finally. "I don't know how to untangle what was strategic from what was real. I don't know if I chose you because you fit or despite you fitting. I just know I chose you."

"That's not good enough." His voice was soft. "I need to know that you wanted me. Not that you chose me. That you actually wanted me for reasons beyond compatibility percentages and long-term planning."

"I do want you—"

"Do you? Or do I just happen to be the most suitable option who was available during your project timeline?"

"That's not fair."

"None of this is fair." He moved to open the door. "I need more time. I need to figure out if I can trust that this is real."

"William, please." She almost told him then. Nearly admitted that she had written in the spreadsheet that he made her laugh, that being with him felt like the first real thing she'd done in years, and that she'd stopped calculating probabilities because nothing about him fit into a spreadsheet.

But his face was so closed off, so hurt. And she was so tired of begging people to believe she was worth the effort.

"I'm sorry," she said instead. "I'm sorry I made the spreadsheet. I'm sorry I kept it. I'm sorry I wasn't brave enough to just let myself fall without a safety net."

"So am I." He held the door open. "I'll see you at the next planning meeting. We still have a presentation to give."

She stepped out into the December chill, and he locked the door behind her.

She got halfway back to the lodge before the tears began.

Dawn found her an hour later, curled up on her bed, staring at the wall.

"I take it the conversation didn't go well."

"He asked if I chose him because he fit my criteria or despite them. And I couldn't answer," Amy's voice was flat. "Because the truth is, I noticed him because he fit. I gave him a chance because the spreadsheet said he was worth investigating. And then I fell for him. But I can't separate the beginning from the rest."

"Did you tell him that?"

"I told him I didn't know. That I couldn't separate strategy from reality." She laughed, but it sounded broken. "He said that wasn't good enough. That he needed to hear I wanted him, not just chose him."

"Do you? Want him?"

"Of course I want him. I want him so badly it scares me. I want him even though he lectures about cobblestones, makes me climb four hundred steps, and challenges every system I try to build. I want him because he makes me laugh, feel safe, and believe I might actually deserve something good."

"Did you tell him that?"

"No."

"Why not?"

"Because his face was so closed off. Because I was so tired of begging. Because I've spent my entire adult life trying to convince people I'm worth the effort, and I couldn't do it one more time."

Dawn sat beside her and took her hand. "You have to tell him the whole truth. Not the careful truth. Not the strategic truth. The messy, vulnerable, I-deleted-the-spreadsheet-because-I-love-you truth."

"What if that makes it worse?"

"What if it makes it better?"

"What if it doesn't matter? What if he's already decided I'm too broken to be worth fixing?"

"Then he's an idiot, and you're better off without him." Dawn squeezed her hand. "But I don't think he's decided that. I think he's scared. I think he's waiting for you to prove this is real."

"How do I prove it?"

"You tell him you love him. Out loud. Not in a text message as damage control. You tell him you love him, you're terrified, and you don't know how to do this without a plan, but you're willing to try."

"That's terrifying."

"Love is frightening. That's what makes it love, not a transaction."

Amy stared at the ceiling, at the water stain in the corner that looked vaguely like a bird, and struggled to find the courage to be that vulnerable.

Her phone Buzzed. Text from William: Gala planning meeting tomorrow at 2 PM. at the community center. We need to finalize the presentation.

She typed back: I'll be there.

Then, before she could stop herself: Can we talk after? Please?

The three dots appeared. Disappeared. Appeared again.

Finally: Maybe. We'll see.

It wasn't a yes. But it wasn't a no.

It was the tiniest sliver of hope, and Amy clung to it like a lifeline.

Tomorrow, she'd tell him everything, the whole messy truth. She'd lay out every fear, every hope, and every moment she'd fallen for him despite trying not to.

She'd tell him she loved him.

And then she'd wait to see if loving him was enough.

Chapter 14
William - December 21st

Physical labor was good for avoiding thought.

William had volunteered for the gala setup mainly because it involved lifting, moving, and arranging, tasks that kept his body busy enough to quiet his mind. He'd been hauling tables and chairs in the community center for two hours, and he'd only managed to think about Amy for most of that time.

So much for distraction.

Jack appeared beside him and grabbed the other end of the table William was trying to maneuver through the doorway. "You look like hell."

"Thanks."

"When's the last time you slept?"

"I sleep."

"For more than three hours at a time?"

William didn't answer, which was answer enough.

They set the table down with the others and stepped back to catch their breath. The community center was gradually turning into a place fit for a Christmas gala, with tables arranged, the stage set, and volunteers on ladders adjusting the lighting.

"Are you going to talk to her?" Jack asked quietly. "Actually talk to her?"

"What's left to say?"

"How about 'I overreacted,' or 'I'm sorry,' or 'I love you too'?"

"She said that in a text message, as damage control, after I caught her treating me like a project."

"She said it because it's true and she was desperate to make you understand." Jack grabbed two more chairs and started arranging them around a table. "You saw the screenshots. You know she was trying to delete the whole thing. You know she chose you over the plan."

"I know she kept the plan as a backup, even after everything."

"Because she was scared. Because you'd told her three days earlier that you were all in, and she was still terrified you'd realize she was too much work and leave." Jack's voice was firm. "She's not Ava. Stop punishing her for what Ava did."

"I'm not—"

"You're used for your appearance. Ava used you for the aesthetic. Amy fell for you despite trying not to. Those aren't the same thing, and you know it."

Before William could reply, Mrs. Peterson showed her unique talent for inserting herself into conversations.

"William, dear. I haven't seen you and Amy together in days. Is everything alright?"

"Everything's fine, Mrs. Peterson."

"It's just that you looked so happy together. And she was so good for you, made you smile more than I've seen in years." Her expression was genuinely concerned, which somehow made it worse. "You're not going to let her go, are you?"

194

"I'm not... we're just figuring some things out."

"Well, figure them out quickly. It's Christmas. No one should be alone during Christmas."

She patted his arm and hurried off, leaving William feeling like he had failed a test given by the town's collective grandmother network.

"The whole town noticed," Jack said. "How good you were together."

"The entire town will notice when we perform at the gala and can barely look at each other."

"That doesn't have to happen. You could fix this."

"How? She made a spreadsheet evaluating me like a project. She had compatibility percentages. Risk assessments. A timeline for when we should hit relationship milestones."

"And she erased everything when she realized she loved you. That's the part you keep ignoring."

Mr. Walters stepped forward next, carrying a box of tablecloths. "William! Good to see you. How's the Wish Box project going?"

"Fine. We're finalizing the presentation."

"You and Amy make a great team. It's a shame you haven't figured out the final clue yet." He set down the box and looked directly at William. "But then, the best things in life can't be solved with logic alone. Sometimes you just have to surrender to the mystery."

He walked away, leaving William with the uneasy feeling that everyone in town could see what he was desperately trying not to admit.

Mayor Karen appeared, clipboard in hand, looking a bit frazzled. "William, thank goodness. Can you help with the stage backdrop? It's—" She stopped, noticing his expression. "Is everything alright? You and Amy haven't had a falling out, have you?"

"We're fine."

"Because the town is really counting on this presentation. And you two have been so wonderful together, solving all those clues and bringing the legend to life." Her smile was hopeful but worried. "You're going to figure it out, aren't you? Both the Wish Box mystery and... whatever else needs figuring?"

"We're working on it."

"Good. That's good." But she looked disappointed, as if she could see the cracks in what they'd built.

William felt it then, the weight of public failure. The entire town had watched them fall for each other, cheered them on, and invested in their story. And now they were about to watch it collapse.

It wasn't just a public failure; it was his failure. His choice to walk away instead of listening. His decision to assume the worst instead of giving her a chance to explain.

His fear outweighing his hope.

He was hauling another table when Peter Alexander showed up, looking uneasy in khakis and a sweater that likely cost more than William's whole wardrobe.

"William, right? We met briefly. I'm Peter. Amy's, well, Amy's ex."

"I remember." William set down the table more firmly than necessary. "What can I do for you?"

"I just wanted to say, look, I know it's none of my business, but I heard you two were having some trouble." Peter shifted his weight awkwardly. "I wanted to apologize for what I said at the market, about her five-year plans and timelines. I was being petty."

"You were being honest."

"I was being an ass. Amy and I didn't work out because I wasn't ready for someone that was so organized, so focused, so..." He searched for the word. "That intentional about building a life. But that's not a flaw. That's just who she is."

"She created a spreadsheet—columns, formulas, and the entire setup."

Peter didn't laugh. "Of course she did. That's not strategy, it's survival. It's her way of saying she still believes in love, even if she's terrified it'll fall apart. And you're pissed because you were on it."

"I'm hurt because I thought what we had was genuine and spontaneous. Not part of her systematic approach to reaching her goals."

"Can I tell you something? In the eight months we dated, Amy tried so hard to be spontaneous for me. Turned off her alarms, stopped making lists, pretended she enjoyed last-minute plans. And it made her miserable. She was anxious all the time, constantly worried she was doing it wrong, exhausting herself trying to be someone she wasn't." Peter looked at him directly. "The fact that she made a spreadsheet doesn't mean she didn't fall for you. It means she fell for you despite being terrified. And for Amy, that's huge."

"She kept it. Even after we, after everything. She kept it as insurance."

"Because she's been taught her whole life that people leave, that love is conditional, and that if she's not perfect, she's not enough," Peter's voice was now firm. "I left her because she was too organized. Her dad left because her mom wasn't perfect enough. Every relationship she's ever had has reinforced the idea that she has to earn love. So yeah, she kept a backup plan. Because that's what you do when you're terrified of losing the one thing you want most."

William wanted to argue. Wanted to insist that keeping a spreadsheet of alternate candidates was not the same as having reasonable fears.

But Peter was right. And William knew it.

"She's not perfect," Peter continued. "She's controlling, neurotic, and probably has seventeen contingency plans for this very conversation. But she's also brilliant, loyal, and brave enough to keep trying even when she's terrified." He paused. "I wasn't good enough for her. I couldn't handle the intensity. But I think maybe you are if you can get past your own fear long enough to see what's actually there."

He walked away, leaving William standing there with a table half-placed and a truth he didn't want to face.

"That looked intense," Jack said, appearing at his side.

"He told me Amy kept the spreadsheet because she's been taught that love is conditional. That everyone in her life has reinforced the idea that she has to be perfect to be worth staying for."

"And?"

"And he's right. And I'm an idiot."

"That's progress."

"I walked away from her, just like her dad did, just like Peter did. I proved every fear she's ever had about not being enough."

"So fix it."

"How?"

"You begin by truly listening when she tries to explain. You realize that her planning and your cynicism are both shields to avoid getting hurt. You decide whether to focus on her flaws or to stay with her despite them."

William looked around the community center, observing the gala preparations, the Christmas decorations, and the town coming together to celebrate a legend about wishes and worthiness.

"I need to think," he said.

"You need to feel," Jack corrected. "Thinking is what got you into this mess."

***

The lighthouse was cold, empty, and just where William needed to be.

He climbed the 412 steps alone this time, no Amy holding his hand, no shared journey to the top. Just him, his thoughts, and the clarity that comes from physical effort.

At the observation deck, he sat where they had kissed, where she had cried, laughed, and said she was terrified and okay all at once.

He tried to sort his feelings.

He was hurt, that much was clear. The spreadsheet felt like a betrayal, like proof that everything they'd built was just calculated, not genuine.

But beneath the hurt was something else. Something he'd been avoiding examining too closely.

He was scared.

Fear that Amy truly loved the real him and that the spreadsheet was just her way of coping with fear. Fear that he'd judged her for planning, while using cynicism for the same reason, to avoid risk.

He was scared that he was sabotaging the best thing that had happened to him in years because being right felt safer than being vulnerable.

Peter's words echoed: *I wasn't good enough for her. I couldn't handle the intensity.*

Was William doing the same thing? Looking for a reason to leave before she could leave him?

He thought about Ava—how she'd used him for appearance, for the story she could tell, for the Instagram version of his life. About how she'd left as soon as something better came along.

Amy wasn't Ava.

Amy had come to Holly Falls with a plan, yes. But she'd also disabled alarms, climbed stairs despite her fear, and told Peter Alexander he was the last man on earth she would consider.

Amy had deleted his compatibility ratings, changed his status from CANDIDATE to NOT A CANDIDATE, and written notes to herself about how he made her feel.

Amy scheduled a final update not to maintain the spreadsheet but to show that she was choosing him.

And he'd walked out before she could explain any of that.

He had judged her for planning while he had been protecting himself with cynicism. Both of them used different tools for the same purpose: avoiding the risk of being hurt.

The final clue came back to him, clear and devastating: *The key is not to seek but to surrender.*

It wasn't about the Wish Box. It had never been about the Wish Box.

It was about them. About releasing control and protection. About surrendering to the frightening possibility that love needs vulnerability, not strategy.

You couldn't unlock love by trying to control it. By planning it. By protecting yourself from it.

You had to surrender to the risk.

The question was simple: Did he want to be right about Amy's flaws, or did he want to be with her despite them?

Did he want to protect himself from potential hurt, or did he want to risk being hurt for the chance at something real?

He sat there as the sun started to set, as the valley below turned gold and then purple and then dark, and tried to find the courage to choose vulnerability over safety.

His phone buzzed. He'd been ignoring it all day, but something made him check.

Two missed calls from Amy. One text, sent three hours ago: *Please. I need to tell you the truth. The whole truth. Not the careful version. When you're ready to listen.*

He stared at the message for a long time.

She'd said "when you're ready." Not "if." Like she knew he'd eventually come around. Like she had more faith in him than he had in himself.

He typed: *I'm sorry for walking out. For not listening. For assuming the worst instead of giving you a chance to explain.*

Deleted it. Too much apology, not enough action.

He typed: *We need to talk. Actually talk. Tomorrow?*

Deleted it. Too vague. Too easy to keep avoiding.

Finally, he typed: *I'll listen when the time comes. I'm not ready yet, but I'm getting there. I promise.*

He sent it before he could second-guess himself.

Her response came immediately: *Thank you. That's all I need. Just a chance to explain.*

Then: *I love you. I know I said it wrong before, in a text as damage control. But I truly mean it. I love you. And I'm scared. And I don't know how to do this without a plan. But I want to try.*

William looked at the words, at her raw honesty, at the vulnerability that must have taken everything for her to type.

He typed back: *I know. I'm scared too.*

It wasn't "I love you too." It wasn't a resolution or a promise or anything close to what she probably needed to hear.

But it was honest. And it was a start.

He climbed back down the four hundred and twelve steps in darkness, using his phone's flashlight to illuminate the way, and tried to figure out how to surrender to something that terrified him.

By the time he got to the bottom, he had made a decision.

He'd talk to her. Tomorrow. Actually talk, actually listen, actually give her the chance to explain without walking out or shutting down or protecting himself with anger.

He would tell her he understood fear because he felt it too. He would tell her he recognized his cynicism as armor because hers was a spreadsheet. He would tell her that maybe they were both too scared to be easy, but that didn't mean they weren't worth the effort.

He'd ask her if she was willing to try being terrified together, if she was open to abandoning the plan and seeing what happens when two scared people choose vulnerability over safety.

And then he'd wait to see if surrender was enough to unlock what they'd built.

Or if some boxes stayed locked, no matter how brave you were willing to be.

Chapter 15
Amy - December 22nd

Amy woke up with hope.

Not the careful, managed optimism she usually cultivated. Real hope. The dangerous kind that made you believe things might actually work out.

William's message from last night sat on her phone: I'll listen when the time comes. I'm not ready yet, but I'm getting there. I promise.

And then: *I know. I'm scared too.*

He was scared too. He wasn't closing the door; he was just asking for some time, and Amy could give him that. She was good at patience when it came with a plan.

She showered and dressed carefully in jeans and her blue sweater, the one William had said made her eyes look green. She put on her grandmother's pearl necklace because it made her feel grounded.

She was about to tell him everything. The full truth. Not the strategic version, not the damage-control version. The messy, humiliating, I-made-a-spreadsheet-because-I-was-terrified version.

She was going to tell him she loved him. Out loud. Looking him in the eyes. No text messages, no qualifications, no safety nets.

She was willing to take the risk.

Her phone buzzed. Text from William: *Town square. 10 AM. By the Wish Box.*

She typed back: *I'll be there.*

Then she grabbed her laptop, planning to show him the app, prove that the spreadsheet was gone, and demonstrate that she had deleted it weeks ago.

She walked to the square, her heart pounding, laptop bag over her shoulder, with her prepared speech replaying in her mind.

William was already there, sitting on the bench facing the Wish Box. He looked tired and guarded. But he stood when he saw her, and that felt significant.

"Hi," she said.

"Hi." He gestured to the bench. "Sit?"

She sat, leaving a space between them that felt like miles.

"Thank you for meeting with me," she said. "Thank you for being willing to listen."

"I said some things I shouldn't have. At the café and at the shop. I was hurt, and I lashed out, and I'm sorry for that."

"You don't need to apologize. You had every right to be hurt." She took a breath, forced herself to meet his eyes. "The spreadsheet was real. PROJECT: CHRISTMAS HUSBAND. I made it before I came here. And yes, you were on it."

He was quiet, but he didn't get up and leave. That was progress.

"I made it because I was terrified. Because I'm twenty-nine, and every relationship I've ever had has ended with someone telling me I'm too much to handle. Because my dad left when I was twelve, and I internalized that if I'd just been better, quieter, easier, more perfect, maybe he would have stayed." Her voice cracked slightly. "Because I thought if I could just approach finding a husband strategically, if I could just optimize for compatibility and minimize risk, I could control the outcome. I could guarantee I wouldn't end up alone."

William's expression was softening. She could see it, the way his shoulders relaxed slightly, the way his eyes gentled.

"So I made a list. Seventeen names. Men who seemed suitable on paper. Men who checked boxes. Men who might tolerate someone as controlling and neurotic as me," she wiped at her eyes, frustrated that she was already crying. "And you were on that list. Candidate number four. Because you were smart, established, had local ties, and seemed like someone who might be worth investigating."

"Amy—"

"Let me finish. Please." She took another breath. "But then I met you. Actually met you. And you lectured me about cobblestones, made me laugh, and caught me in a basement when I was scared. Suddenly, the spreadsheet stopped making sense; the criteria no longer mattered. The entire systematic approach felt pointless because you made me want to throw the plan away and just see what happened."

"So you deleted it."

"I tried to. I deleted parts of it. I turned off the alarms. I stopped updating it. But I couldn't completely delete it because—" She stopped, shame flooding through her. "Because I was terrified. Because what if you realized I was too much to handle and left? What if this didn't work out? I needed to know I had options. I needed insurance."

"Insurance against me leaving."

"Insurance against being alone."

They sat in silence for a moment. William was processing, she could see him working through it, trying to understand.

"I have proof," she said suddenly. "That I deleted most of it. That I stopped treating you like a candidate weeks ago. I can show you, it's on my laptop—"

"You brought your laptop to prove you deleted a spreadsheet about me?"

"I brought proof that I chose you. That I stopped seeing you as a project and started seeing you as… " she paused, "as the person I love. As the person I want. Not because you check boxes but because you make me believe I might actually deserve something good."

She pulled her laptop from her bag, opened it, and navigated to the spreadsheet app.

"See? It's gone. The whole thing. I deleted it after the lighthouse. After you kissed me and told me I was enough. I deleted everything because I no longer needed it. I didn't want it anymore."

She showed him the app and the empty space where the spreadsheet used to be.

William leaned in closer, examining the screen. Then his eyes shifted to the recently-opened files list at the bottom.

"What's that?" He pointed.

Amy's stomach dropped.

There, in the recently-opened files: *PROJECT_CHRISTMAS_ HUSBAND_BACKUP.xlsx*

"That's—" She tried to close the laptop. "That's nothing. That's just— "

"A backup." His voice had gone flat. "You kept a backup."

"I forgot about it. I didn't, it was automatic cloud backup, I didn't know it was there—"

"Can I see it?"

"William, it's not, it's the old version, from before—"

"Can I see it, Amy?"

She hesitated, and that hesitation proved to be fatal. She knew it was deadly even as it happened, understood she should just show him right away, but the shame was too much, her hands trembled, and she couldn't quite bring herself to open the file she knew would destroy everything.

"Please," he said quietly. "If you want me to trust you, show me."

She opened the file.

The spreadsheet revealed all its clinical and humiliating details: seventeen names listed alphabetically, with columns for age, occupation, compatibility probability, risk assessment, and timeline recommendations.

And there, in row four:

William Crane, 32, Historian/Business Owner

He took the laptop from her hands, scrolled down to read the full entry.

She watched his face as he read, saw hope fade, and saw softness turn back into pain.

"Read it to me," he said, his voice dangerously quiet. "I want to hear you read what you wrote about me."

"William, please—"

"Read it."

Her hands were shaking so badly she could barely scroll. "Candidate number four. William Crane. Strengths: Local ties, intelligent, good with hands—" She stopped, choking on the words.

"Keep going."

"—verified via observation of shelf repair, December third. Weaknesses: Excessive cynicism regarding holiday traditions. Resistance to planning. Status: Active Pursuit." She was crying openly now. "Notes: Strong physical attraction. Potential long-term compatibility pending further assessment. Decision point: December fourteenth."

The silence that followed was devastating.

"December fourteenth," William repeated. "That's the day we kissed on the lighthouse. The day you cried and said you were terrified and so okay."

"It was before, that entry was from before, I wrote it the day after we met, before I knew you—"

"You had a decision point for whether I was worth keeping."

"That's not what it meant.

"You verified I was good with my hands by observation." He looked at her, and his eyes were empty. "Like I was a potential hire. Like you were checking my qualifications."

"I know how it sounds.

"You evaluated my long-term compatibility. You scheduled a decision point for the same day we had our first kiss." He stood, handed her back the laptop. "I was right the first time. You don't see people. You see projects."

"That's not true.

"Isn't it? You're a consultant who specializes in strategic life planning. You approached finding a husband the same way you'd approach optimizing a client's five-year business plan. I was just another objective to achieve."

"You were never just—" She was sobbing now, barely able to speak. "I deleted it. I chose you. I chose the real you."

"When?" He stepped back from her, creating distance. "When did you choose me, Amy? Was it before or after you checked all your boxes? Before or after you confirmed I met your criteria? Before or after your decision point proved I was worth keeping?"

"It wasn't like that."

"Then what was it like? Explain it to me in a way that doesn't make me feel like I've been just another item on your checklist for the past three weeks."

She couldn't. She stood there with tears streaming down her face, holding her laptop, and no words that could fix this.

"I love you," she tried. "I know that doesn't mean anything right now, but I love you. Not candidate number four. You. William Crane who lectures about cobblestones and makes me laugh and made me believe I could be messy without being abandoned—"

"But you kept the backup. Even after the lighthouse. Even after I told you that you were enough. You kept it."

"I forgot about it."

"You're a consultant who specializes in strategic planning. You don't forget about backup files." His voice was quiet now, defeated. "You kept it because some part of you was still treating this like a project. Still maintaining your options. Still making sure you had an exit strategy if I didn't work out."

"That's not—" but it was. Some part of her had kept it. Some scared, desperate part that couldn't quite believe this was real.

"I need to go." He was already preparing to walk away. "We still have to present at the gala. Christmas Eve. I'll meet you there. We'll fulfill our professional obligation to the town. And then—"

"And then what?"

"And then I don't know." He stopped and turned back. "I wanted to believe you. I wanted to believe the spreadsheet was just fear, just armor, just you being scared. But you kept a backup. You documented me like I was a research subject. You scheduled a decision point for the day we kissed."

"William, please."

"I can't do this." He walked away, leaving her standing alone in the town square with her laptop and her backup file and the wreckage of everything they'd built.

Amy stood there for a long moment, unable to move. Unable to process what had just happened.

Townspeople were staring. Mrs. Peterson approached, her face showing concern. "Amy, dear? Are you alright?"

"I'm fine." The words escaped automatically, a line she had perfected over years of pretending everything was under control. "Everything's fine."

"It doesn't look fine."

"I'm fine. Thank you. Please, excuse me." She walked away before Mrs. Peterson could say anything else.

She reached the edge of the square before her legs gave out. She sat on a bench facing the Wish Box, that stupid, locked, legendary box that promised wishes to those who proved themselves worthy.

She had tried to prove herself worthy, to plan her way to love, and to organize her path to happiness.

And all she'd done was prove William right. She didn't see people. She saw projects. She saw objectives to accomplish, risks to handle, and compatibility metrics to optimize.

She had reduced him to just a line item. To a candidate. To a decision point on December 14th.

The day they'd kissed, she was reminded to decide if he was worth keeping.

God. No wonder he'd left.

She sat there as the December cold seeped into her bones, while the morning shoppers gave her pitying looks, and the Christmas lights mocked her with their cheerful glow.

The Wish Box sat there, locked and silent. A reminder that some people were worthy of wishes while other people just broke everything they touched.

Her phone buzzed. Dawn: *Where are you? Are you okay?*

Amy typed back: *Town square. Not okay.*

Dawn appeared ten minutes later, looked at Amy's face, and then wrapped her arms around her.

"What happened?"

"He saw the backup file. The original spreadsheet. With all the notes. The compatibility assessments. The decision point scheduled for the day we kissed."

"Oh, Amy."

"I told him I forgot about it. That it was an automatic cloud backup. But he's right, I'm a strategic planner. I don't forget about backup files. Some part of me kept it. Some scared part that couldn't quite believe this was real."

"Did you explain? Did you tell him you deleted everything else?"

"I tried. He didn't want to hear it. He just kept saying I'd verified he was good with his hands, as if he was a potential hire. That I'd scheduled a decision point to see if he was worth keeping." She laughed, but it came out broken. "He's right. That's exactly what I did. I treated him like a project."

"At first. But then you fell for him. Really fell for him."

"Doesn't matter. I had a backup file. I kept options. I maintained an exit strategy." She pulled away from Dawn, wiped her face. "I'm going back to the lodge. I need to, I don't know. Cry. Delete everything. Figure out how to present at the gala without falling apart."

"Amy—"

"I lost him. I lost him because I couldn't just let myself fall without a safety net. Because I'm so terrified of being alone that I guaranteed I would be."

She walked back to the lodge in a daze, feeling numb except for the pain in her chest that seemed like something vital had been torn out.

In her room, she opened her laptop. Stared at the backup file.

She should delete it. She should have done it weeks ago. She never should have made it in the first place.

Instead, she simply closed the laptop, lay down on her bed, and tried to figure out how you managed to survive losing something you never truly had a right to in the first place.

Her phone buzzed. Text from William: *Gala presentation is at 7 PM on Christmas Eve. I'll meet you there at 6:30 to review. This is for professional purposes only. Please don't try to contact me before then.*

She typed back: *Understood.*

Then she turned off her phone, pulled the covers over her head, and let the numbness take control. Because feeling was too dangerous. Feeling was how you got hurt. Feeling was how you ended up alone with a backup file, a broken heart, and a wish box that had nothing to give you.

She'd tried to plan her way to love.

All she had was proof that some people weren't meant to have their wishes granted.

Chapter 16
William - December 23rd

William had cleaned his shop three times in the past twelve hours.

The first time, at midnight, was somewhat justified; there was actual dust on the shelves and real disorder in the filing system. The second time, at 4 AM when sleep was impossible, was excessive but understandable.

The third time, at 9 AM, was just rage given physical form.

He was currently attacking a display case that had been spotless yesterday with a cleaning cloth and the sort of vigor usually reserved for removing crime scene evidence.

Jack said from the doorway, "You're going to rub the finish off that wood."

William didn't stop. "It needs cleaning."

"It was clean yesterday. I was here. I saw it." Jack walked in, pulled up a stool. "You look like you're trying to alphabetize your feelings."

"My feelings are fine."

"Your feelings are destroying antique furniture."

William threw the cloth down and moved to reorganize a shelf of books that were already sorted by date, author, and subject matter. "She made me a line item, Jack. A candidate. Candidate number four."

"I know."

She observed that I was skilled with my hands, as if I were a potential candidate. He took out a book and placed it back exactly where it was. "She had criteria. Compatibility metrics. A decision point scheduled for the day we kissed."

"I know."

She treated finding a husband like a business deal. Like I was a project to optimize. He was reorganizing faster now, pulling books out and putting them back in the same spots, accomplishing nothing except channeling fury into motion. "And even after everything, after the chapel, after the lighthouse, after I told her she was enough, she kept a backup file. She maintained her options. She—"

A book slipped from his hand, knocked into three others, and sent them tumbling to the floor in a domino effect that left William standing there, surrounded by leather-bound volumes and his frustration.

"You done?" Jack asked mildly.

"No. I'm not finished. I'm—" William paused, glancing at the books scattered on the floor, at the cleaning cloth he'd thrown, at the perfectly organized shop he'd been destroying with frantic tidying. "I'm being ridiculous."

"Little bit."

"She made a spreadsheet."

"She did."

"With my name on it."

"Yep."

"And you're not outraged on my behalf?"

"I'm outraged enough to drive over here at 9 AM on a Saturday to make sure you don't rage-clean yourself into a heart attack." Jack leaned back against the counter. "But I'm also clear-eyed enough to recognize that you're hurt, you're scared, and you're doing that thing where you convince yourself being angry is easier than being vulnerable."

"She treated me like a project."

"She was scared. You were scared. You both chose armor. Hers was a spreadsheet. Yours was being right about why relationships fail. Jack's voice was gentle but firm. "Hurt people hurt people. The question is, do you love her?"

William wanted to argue. He wanted to insist that love was irrelevant when trust was broken. He wanted to maintain the righteous anger that felt safer than the grief underneath.

Instead, he just went quiet.

"You do," Jack said. It wasn't a question.

"That doesn't change what she did."

"Doesn't change what you want, either."

William bent down to pick up the scattered books, needing something to do with his hands. "I love her. Even now. Even angry. Even knowing she had a backup file, a decision point, and a list of seventeen other candidates. I love her."

"So what are you going to do about it?"

"I don't know. Loving someone doesn't mean trusting them. Doesn't mean believing they won't hurt you again."

"True. But it also means deciding whether the pain is worth the risk." Jack helped him gather the books and stack them on the counter. "Ava hurt you because she used you. Amy hurt you because she was protecting herself. Those aren't the same thing."

"Feel the same."

"I know. But they're not."

The shop door swung open. Lily hurried inside, heading straight for William with the focused determination of a five-year-old on a mission.

"William!" She crashed into his legs, hugged them. "Daddy says you're sad."

"I'm fine, Lily-pad."

"You don't look fine. You look like when I'm sad about my fish." She looked up at him with those huge eyes that made lying impossible. "Is Miss Amy sad too?"

"Probably."

"You should hug her. Hugs fix sad."

William's throat tightened. "It's more complicated than that, sweetheart."

"Why?"

"Because sometimes grown-ups hurt each other's feelings, and a hug doesn't automatically fix that."

"But it helps, right? When I hurt Daddy's feelings by accident, I say sorry and give hugs, and then he's not sad anymore."

"That's because your daddy is a better person than I am."

Jack made a sound that might have been disagreement.

Lily wasn't finished. "Miss Amy is really nice. She helped me make cookies and didn't get mad when I spilled flour everywhere. And she makes you smile with the happy smile, not the polite smile."

"The happy smile?"

"You have two smiles. The polite one you use for strangers and the happy one you use for people you really like. You use the happy one with Miss Amy," she said with the certainty of a child who'd been watching adults her whole life. "If she makes you smile the happy smile, you should hug her when she's sad."

She released his legs, hurried over to examine a box of old photographs, leaving William standing there, feeling as if he'd just received life advice from someone who still believed in Santa Claus.

"Out of the mouths of babes," Jack said quietly.

"She's five."

She's five and has figured out what you're still pretending not to see. You love Amy. Amy loves you. You're both scared and hurt, and you're making it worse by trying to protect yourselves."

"It's not that simple."

"Isn't it?" Jack pulled Lily away from a box she was about to tip over, settled her with a stack of old postcards to look through. "Dawn's doing the same thing Amy did. Running because staying feels too dangerous. Keeping her apartment in Portland as insurance. Making exit plans while telling me she wants to stay."

"That's different—"

"Is it? Amy kept a spreadsheet. Dawn kept a lease. Both of them are trying to protect themselves from getting hurt by guaranteeing they have an escape route." He looked at William directly. "And you're doing the same thing by staying angry. By focusing on the spreadsheet instead of acknowledging that she deleted it. By punishing her for having fear instead of recognizing that fear is just love without trust."

"She scheduled a decision point for the day we kissed."

"She set a reminder to record that she was choosing you over the plan. But you didn't let her explain that part. You just saw the date and assumed the worst."

William wanted to argue. Wanted to insist that his interpretation was the only reasonable one.

But he kept seeing Amy's face in the town square. The way she'd tried to explain. The way she'd said "it was before," "I deleted it," and "I chose you."

The way he'd walked away without letting her finish.

"I'm punishing her for what Ava did," he said quietly.

"Little bit."

"Ava used me for the aesthetics. Amy fell for me even though she tried not to. Those aren't the same thing."

"No, they're not."

"But Amy still kept the backup file, maintained options, and treated this like a project she could optimize."

"Or she kept the backup file because everyone in her life has taught her that love is conditional. That if she's not perfect, she's not enough. That planning is the only way to feel safe." Jack's voice was gentle now. "She made a spreadsheet because she's terrified. You stayed angry because you're terrified. Neither of those things means you don't love each other."

Lily appeared at William's elbow, holding up a postcard. "What's this say?"

William looked at the faded writing. "'Wish you were here.' It's what people write when they're away from someone they miss."

"Like you miss Miss Amy?"

He started to deny it, but the lie wouldn't come. "Yeah. Like I miss Miss Amy."

"Then go see her," Lily said it with the simple logic of someone who'd never had her heart broken. "If you miss someone, you go see them. That's how it works."

"I can't. Not yet."

"Why not?"

"Because I'm still hurt. And angry. And I don't know if I can trust her not to hurt me again."

"But if you love her, you have to try. That's what Daddy says. Love means trying even when it's hard."

Jack picked her up and settled her on his hip. "I may have been editorializing our conversations about Dawn."

"You've been using your five-year-old as a relationship counselor?"

"She's very wise for her age." Jack adjusted Lily higher. "But she's right. Love means trying even when it's tough. Even when you're scared. Even when the other person has hurt you."

"What if she hurts me again?"

"Then you'll have learned something. But at least you'll have tried."

"What do I want, Jack? To be right about her flaws, or to be with her despite them?"

"That's the question, isn't it?" Jack headed for the door, Lily waving over his shoulder. "Only you can answer it. But I'd suggest you figure it out soon. The gala's tomorrow night. The town's counting on you both to present. And from what Dawn tells me, Amy's not doing much better than you are."

They left, and William stood in his shop surrounded by overly clean surfaces and reorganized shelves, with the question he'd been avoiding.

What did he want?

221

He wanted Amy to have never made the spreadsheet. Wanted her to have fallen for him spontaneously, completely, without any strategic planning, risk assessment, or backup files.

But that wasn't who Amy was. Amy was spreadsheets, color-coded calendars, and careful risk management. Amy understood that love was conditional, and planning was the only way to feel safe.

And he'd fallen for her anyway, despite everything: the spreadsheet, the alarms, and the organizational systems that made no sense to anyone but her.

He'd fallen for Amy Donovan exactly as she was.

The question was whether loving her was enough to forgive her for being scared.

His phone rang. Mayor Karen.

William, I'm just confirming, you and Amy presenting tomorrow night at seven? The town is so excited, and ticket sales are incredible. Everyone wants to know if you solved the final clue.

"We'll be there."

"Both of you?"

"Both of us. Professionally."

"Oh." Karen's disappointment was audible. "I'd hoped, well, the town was really rooting for you two. You seemed so happy together."

"Things change."

"They don't have to. It's Christmas, William. Time for miracles and second chances and—"

"We'll present at seven, Mayor. I have to go."

He hung up and immediately felt guilty for his brusqueness. Karen didn't deserve his bad mood.

Nobody else really deserved his bad mood, maybe just himself.

He glanced at his phone. No messages from Amy. She respected his request not to reach out before the gala.

Which meant if he wanted to fix this, he had to be the one to reach out.

Did he want to fix it?

He thought about Lily's wisdom. *If you love her, you have to try.*

He thought about Jack's question. *To be right, or to be with her?*

He thought about Amy in the town square, laptop open, trying to show him she'd deleted everything. The way she'd said "I chose you" like it was both a surrender and a victory.

He pulled up his texts, started typing.

We need to talk before the gala. Not just about the presentation. About us.

Deleted it. Too vague.

I'm still angry. But I'm also willing to listen. Really listen this time.

Deleted it—too many steps.

Finally: *Coffee? Tomorrow morning, before the gala? I think we both owe it to ourselves to actually talk instead of just hurting each other.*

He sent it before he could second-guess himself.

Her response came five minutes later: *Yes. Bean Counter at 9?*

I'll be there.

He put down his phone, glanced around his overly clean shop, and tried to figure out how to have a conversation that might save what they'd built or completely destroy it.

He was still angry. Still hurt. Still questioning whether he could trust her.

But Lily was right. If you loved someone, you had to try.

Even when it was hard. Even when you were scared. Even when trying meant risking getting hurt again.

Tomorrow he'll try.

Tonight, he'd simply sit with the anger, love, and fear all mixed together, hoping that was enough to find his way through.

Chapter 17
Amy - December 23rd

Amy hadn't left her room in thirty-six hours.

She'd heard Dawn knocking yesterday, sensing the concern in her sister's voice calling through the door. She also heard her retreat when it became clear Amy wasn't going to answer.

She hadn't ordered anything from room service. Hadn't eaten anything. She just lay in bed, staring at the ceiling, at the water stain that looked like a bird, trying to figure out how you survived being exactly what you'd always feared you were.

Too broken to love. Too complicated to hold onto. Too fundamentally flawed to deserve something good.

The knocking resumed. Dawn's voice: "Amy, I'm coming in. I have the spare key from the front desk, and I'm using it."

Amy didn't move.

The door opened. Dawn stepped inside, took one look at Amy on the bed, and her face crumpled.

"Oh, honey." She closed the door, crossed to the bed, and sat on the edge. "How bad is it?"

"He read the entire document. The original spreadsheet. With all the notes. The compatibility assessment. The decision point is scheduled for December 14th." Amy's voice was flat, empty. "He made me read it out loud. Made me say the words 'verified via observation' about his hands. Made me explain that I'd scheduled a decision to keep him for the same day we kissed."

"Amy—"

"And you know what the worst part is? He was right. I assessed him like a project. I did verify his qualifications. I did schedule a decision point. The spreadsheet wasn't just fear; it was me treating a human being like a line item on a business plan."

Dawn lay down beside her, both of them staring at the ceiling. "You fell for him, though. Really fell for him."

"Doesn't matter. The falling happened after the assessment. After I'd determined he was worth investigating. I can't separate the beginning from the rest, and he knows it."

"What did he say?"

"He said I was approaching finding a husband like a business deal, that I didn't see people, only projects. And he..." Her voice broke. "He said I'd proved him right."

They lay there in silence for a long moment.

"Jack asked me to spend Christmas with his family," Dawn said quietly. "Real Christmas. With his parents and Lily and everyone. Asked me to be part of it. To start building something real."

"What did you say?"

"I said I'm leaving on the 26th, just as I planned. That this was always meant to be temporary. That I never promised to stay." Dawn's voice was thick. "And Lily started crying. And Jack looked at me like I was a monster. And I ran, because that's what I do. I run before anyone can leave me first."

Amy turned her head and looked at her sister. Really looked at her. Saw the same fear, the same wound, the same desperate attempt at protection.

"But I don't think it's about the spreadsheet," Amy said slowly. "I think it's about what it reminded him of. He told me once, barely, about an engagement that ended when his fiancée called him 'emotionally unavailable.' Maybe seeing my checklist felt like reliving that."

"We're doing the same thing," she said. "You're running. I'm planning. Both of us are trying to control the outcome so we don't get hurt."

"And we're both getting hurt anyway."

"Because the thing we're most afraid of, being abandoned, is the thing we're guaranteeing by protecting ourselves."

Dawn rolled onto her side and faced Amy. "When did we become so scared?"

"I think we've always been scared. We just became really good at pretending we weren't."

"When Mom and Dad divorced—" Dawn stopped, swallowed hard. "Do you remember what Mom said? That day when she was packing Dad's things?"

Amy remembered. She had been twelve. Dawn had been twelve. They had both been sitting on the stairs listening to their mother cry in the bedroom.

"She said if she'd been better, he would've stayed."

She said if she had been less demanding, less emotional, and not so much, maybe he wouldn't have needed to leave.

"She said love was something you earned. That you had to be good enough, perfect enough, easy enough to prevent someone from leaving."

They'd absorbed that lesson. Internalized it. Let it shape every relationship they've had since.

Amy had learned that she needed to be perfect. That if she could just be organized enough, competent enough, low-maintenance enough, maybe someone would want to stay.

Dawn had learned that staying was risky. That if you never committed, never rooted, never let anyone get close enough to matter, they couldn't hurt you when they left.

Same wound. Different symptoms.

"I made the spreadsheet," Amy said, "because I thought if I was strategic enough, I could avoid being left. I could control who I fell for, when I fell for them, and how deep I let it go. But all I did was become the person who leaves first, by never really arriving."

"I kept moving," Dawn said, "so I would never have to watch someone walk away. But I am the one walking. Every single time. I'm the one leaving Jack and Lily even though I love them, because leaving feels safer than being left."

"How do we stop?"

"I don't know." Dawn reached for Amy's hand and held it tightly. "But I think we have to try. I think we have to be brave enough to want things, even if wanting them might destroy us."

"That's terrifying."

"Love is terrifying. That's what makes it love."

They lay there holding hands, two sisters who had spent their lives protecting themselves, both realizing that their protection had become a prison.

"I've spent my whole life trying to control love. Quantify it. Protect myself from it. But love doesn't work that way." Amy looked at Dawn.

"Tomorrow, I tell him everything. Not to win him back. Just to stop hiding."

"Will he listen?"

"I don't know. But I have to try. I need to show up tomorrow and tell him everything, the divorce, the wound, the reason I made the spreadsheet, and hope that's enough."

"And if it's not enough?"

"Then at least I'll know I was brave. At least I'll know I tried." She squeezed Dawn's hand. "What about you? Are you going to stay?"

"I'm terrified of staying."

"That's not an answer."

"I know." Dawn was quiet for a long moment. "Jack deserves someone brave enough to choose him. Lily deserves someone who won't run when things get hard. And I want to be that person, but I don't know if I can."

"You can. You're the bravest person I know. You've traveled the world alone, built a life from nothing, made friends everywhere you go. That's not the resume of a coward."

"That's the resume of someone avoiding commitment."

"Or the story of someone learning to be brave in different ways." Amy turned onto her side, facing her sister. "You can also learn to be brave by staying. I know you can."

"What if I mess it up? What if I stay and it doesn't work and I end up hurting them more by giving them hope?"

"What if you stay and it actually works? What if staying is how you discover you've been brave enough all along?"

Dawn's eyes filled with tears. "Tomorrow. Christmas Eve. We both show up for real. No running, no planning, no safety nets. Just truth."

"Just truth," Amy agreed.

They held each other as the afternoon light faded, two sisters making a pact to be brave and trying to believe that bravery was enough.

After Dawn left, Amy sat up. Looked at her laptop sitting on the desk, closed and silent.

She opened it. Navigated to her cloud storage. Found the backup file.

PROJECT_CHRISTMAS_HUSBAND_BACKUP.xlsx

She looked at it for a long moment. This file had ruined everything. This detailed, clinical record of her fear had cost her the person she loved most.

She should have deleted it weeks ago. She should have trusted that what she and William had was real. She should have been brave enough to let go of the safety net. But she hadn't. She'd kept it. Maintained it. Let it sit there as insurance against her worst fears.

And in keeping it, she'd guaranteed those fears would come true.

She searched her entire computer and found three more backups: one in her desktop folder labeled "PERSONAL," one in her documents, and one in her downloads from when she emailed it to herself weeks ago.

Four copies. Four safety nets. Four pieces of evidence that she had never fully committed to surrendering control.

She selected the first one and hovered the mouse over "delete."

Her hand trembled.

This was it. This was the moment. Delete these files, and she would have nothing left, no backup plan, no exit strategy, no way to protect herself if this didn't work out with William.

Simply vulnerability. Simply trust. Simply the frightening idea that maybe love doesn't need a safety net.

She clicked delete.

The file disappeared.

She found the second one. Deleted it.

The third. Deleted.

The fourth. Deleted.

Then she opened her trash folder, where all deleted files are stored temporarily before being permanently erased.

She could still recover them. She could still maintain her options. She could still have insurance.

She selected "Empty Trash."

The computer asked if she was sure, warned her that this action was permanent, and told her these files would be gone forever.

"I'm sure," she whispered, and clicked "Yes."

The files are gone. Truly vanished. No way to recover them. No backup of a backup. Just gone.

Amy sat there staring at the empty trash folder, feeling like she had just jumped off a cliff without knowing if there was water below.

No safety net. No insurance. No way to protect herself from the fall.

Just the choice to fall and hope someone would catch her.

Or the choice to fall and accept that she might crash, but at least she'd been brave enough to try.

She closed the laptop. Put on her coat. Walked out into the December evening.

The town square was quiet, with most people at home with their families preparing for Christmas Eve tomorrow. The shops were closed, the lights twinkling, and the Wish Box sat in its usual place, locked, silent, and legendary.

Amy walked up to it. Stood in front of it. Laid her hand on the cold metal.

"I don't know how to surrender," she said quietly. "I've spent my entire life learning how to control, how to plan, how to protect myself from uncertainty. And now I'm standing here with no plan, no safety net, and no idea if any of this will work out."

The Wish Box didn't answer, open, or offer any magical solutions.

But Amy still heard the final clue, ringing in her mind: The key is not to seek but to surrender.

She understood now. The Wish Box didn't open because you solved riddles, followed clues, or approached it strategically. It opened when you stopped trying to control the outcome, when you were brave enough to want something without any guarantee of getting it.

When you took a risk.

Tomorrow, she would stand before the entire town to present her findings. Tomorrow, she would tell William everything—the divorce, the wound, the spreadsheet, the fear. Tomorrow, she would surrender control and hope that vulnerability was enough.

She was terrified.

But she was finally finished running, finished planning, and finished trying to organize her path to happiness.

Tomorrow, she would simply be honest. Tomorrow, she would just be brave.

Tomorrow she'd discover if surrender was the missing piece all along.

She walked back to the lodge as snow began to fall, tiny flakes catching in her hair and melting on her coat. The Christmas lights blurred through her tears, and she let herself cry as she walked because crying was honest, and maybe honesty was all she had left.

In her room, she pulled out her phone and saw William's message from earlier: *'Coffee? Tomorrow morning before the gala?' She thought we both owe it to ourselves to actually talk instead of just hurting each other.*

She had already agreed, but now she needed to add something.

She typed: *I deleted everything. All the backups. Every safety net. I'm showing up tomorrow with just the truth. I hope that's enough.*

She sent it before she had a chance to second-guess herself.

His response came five minutes later: *It's a start.*

Not "I forgive you." Not "I love you too." Just "It's a start."

But a start was more than she had an hour ago. A start meant possibility. Meant maybe. Meant the door wasn't entirely closed. And, she would take it.

She changed into pajamas, climbed into bed, and tried to sleep, knowing that tomorrow would be either the day she got everything she wanted or the day she lost it all.

Either way, she'd be brave.

Either way, she'd show up.

Either way, she'd finally stop running from the one thing she wanted most.

Even if wanting it broke her heart.

Chapter 18
William - December 23rd

William couldn't sleep.

He'd tried. Gone through all the motions, pajamas, teeth brushing, bed. Laid there staring into the darkness as his mind replayed the town square scene on endless repeat.

Amy's face when he made her read the spreadsheet aloud. The way her voice broke on "verified via observation." The way she tried to explain, and he shut her down. The way she said "I love you," and he walked away.

He'd wanted her to hurt. Wanted her to feel what he felt, the betrayal, the humiliation, the devastating realization that maybe you weren't actually wanted for who you were.

He'd succeeded. She'd been destroyed.

And now he felt sick about it.

He got up at seven, gave up on sleep, and went downstairs to make coffee. Found an envelope that had been slipped under the shop door sometime during the day.

His name is on the front in careful handwriting. Amy's handwriting.

He opened it.

William,

I don't expect forgiveness. I know what the spreadsheet looked like. I know what I did. I know I hurt you in ways that apologies can't fix.

I just need you to know: I didn't fall for candidate #4. I fell for the man who made me forget numbers existed. I fell for you.

I fell for the way you lecture about cobblestones like they're the most important thing in the world. For the way you made me climb four hundred and twelve steps, even though I was terrified. For the way you see the value in preserving small details that everyone else overlooks.

I fell for you because you made me laugh when I was planning my response. Because you caught me in a basement when I was scared. Because you told me I didn't have to earn this.

The spreadsheet was fear. It was armor. It was me trying to control something that can't be controlled. But what I felt for you, what I feel for you, was never part of any plan.

I'm sorry I didn't trust that sooner. I'm sorry I kept the backup file. I'm sorry I hurt you. You deserved better. You deserved real.

I'm trying to learn how.

—A

William read it three times.

The fourth time, his eyes blurred. His head dropped forward. He pressed his hands to his face and tried to breathe through the overwhelming wave of emotion.

No longer angry. Just a mix of hurt and disappointment. Grief for the time they'd wasted. Grief for the hurt they'd caused each other. Grief for two scared people who both chose protection over vulnerability.

They could have had this conversation a week ago. It could have been honest instead of defensive. They could have chosen each other instead of hiding behind pride.

Instead, they both remained scared. Both stayed safe. Both proved exactly what they feared: that they weren't brave enough for love.

He carefully folded the letter and placed it in his pocket.

His grandfather's pocket watch sat on the counter where he left it that morning. William picked it up and ran his thumb over the worn brass.

His grandfather had given it to him the year before he died. Had said, "Love isn't about being right. It's about showing up even when you're wrong."

William was twenty-two and believed he understood. Believed love was about grand gestures, perfect timing, and being the person who didn't make mistakes.

Now he was thirty-four and understood that love meant showing up regardless. It's about being wrong, scared, flawed, and choosing vulnerability over safety.

He pocketed the watch, grabbed his coat, and headed out.

The lighthouse climb was easier in the evening than it would have been at night, still some twilight left, enough to see the path and avoid breaking his neck on the uneven trail.

He climbed the 412 steps alone, with no Amy gripping his hand or sharing the journey. Just him, his thoughts, and the clear focus that came from physical effort.

At the observation deck, he sat where they'd kissed, where she'd cried tears of joy and fear, and where he'd told her she was enough and meant every word.

The valley stretched out below him, with Holly Falls shining bright with Christmas lights, and William tried to figure out what he truly wanted.

He could protect his heart. He could stay angry. He could maintain that she hurt him too badly to forgive. He could walk away and never risk being hurt like this again.

Protection was safe. Protection was comfortable. It was what he'd been doing for three years since Ava left.

And protection had caused him misery.

Or he could give his heart to Amy. Could choose to believe her letter. Could accept that the spreadsheet was fear, not manipulation. Could trust that she'd fallen for him despite trying not to.

Giving his heart to her was terrifying. She might hurt him again. She might have other safety nets he doesn't know about. She might decide he's too much work after all.

But giving his heart to her was also the only way to get what he truly wanted.

The question was straightforward: Did he want to be correct about her flaws, or did he want to be with her despite them?

Did he prefer being safe over loving Amy Donovan?

He sat there as the sun finished setting, the stars appeared, the December cold seeped through his coat, and he made his choice.

He forgave her.

Not because what she'd done was okay. Not because the spreadsheet didn't hurt. Not because scheduling a decision point for the day they kissed wasn't devastating.

He forgave her because he loved her more than he loved being right.

He forgave her because she was scared, and he understood what fear was. Because she tried to protect herself, and he responded with cynicism. Because they were both flawed people doing flawed things, and maybe that was okay.

He forgave her because the alternative, staying angry, staying safe, staying alone, was worse than the risk of being hurt again.

He pulled out his phone and looked at her text from earlier: I deleted everything. All the backups. Every safety net. I'm showing up tomorrow with just the truth. I hope that's enough.

She had deleted all the spreadsheets. She chose vulnerability over safety. She surrendered the plan.

Now it was his turn.

The final clue was revealed to him: The key isn't to seek but to surrender.

Amy had to let go of control. Release the planning, safety nets, and the desperate need to manage every outcome.

He had to let go of the need to be right. Release his anger, his hurt, and his desperate urge to protect himself from being hurt or used again.

That's how the Wish Box opened. That's how love worked.

Mutual vulnerability. Mutual surrender. Two scared people choosing each other despite the risk.

He would tell her tomorrow, before the gala, during their coffee meeting. He would tell her he understood, that he forgave her. That he wanted to try again.

This time, with honesty. This time, without spreadsheets or cynicism. This time, just two terrified people showing up anyway.

He climbed back down the 412 steps in complete darkness, using his phone's flashlight, and tried not to think about how many ways this could still go wrong.

She might not forgive him for walking away. She might decide he was too quick to anger, too judgmental, and too willing to assume the worst. She might conclude she was better off with someone who didn't punish her for being scared.

Or she might show up tomorrow and pick him. Pick vulnerability. Pick the terrifying possibility that maybe they could build something real.

Either way, he'd be brave enough to try. Either way, he'd surrender.

Back in his apartment, William tried to sleep but failed spectacularly. His mind kept replaying what he'd say tomorrow.

I forgive you felt too simple.

I understand why you made the spreadsheet felt too clinical.

I love you felt too vulnerable when he didn't know if she still loved him back.

Finally, around midnight, he settled on the truth: *I was scared, too. Let's try being scared together.*

He'd say that. Tomorrow. At coffee, before the gala presentation that could either be the most awkward public appearance of their lives or the start of something new.

His phone buzzed. Text from Jack: *Dawn told me Amy deleted all the spreadsheets. That she's showing up tomorrow with just truth. Thought you should know.*

William responded: I know. I'm ready to listen.

Good. She deserves that. You both do.

William put down his phone, took out Amy's letter, and read it once more.

I didn't fall for candidate #4. I fell for the man who made me forget that numbers existed.

He had been so focused on the spreadsheet, on the pain, betrayal, and clinical documentation of his worth that he missed what she was really saying.

She'd fallen for him despite trying not to, despite the plan, despite every organizational instinct screaming at her to stay safe.

She had surrendered first, weeks ago, and he had been too hurt to notice.

Tomorrow, he would tell her. Tomorrow, he would surrender as well.

Tomorrow, they'd discover if mutual vulnerability was enough to unlock what they nearly lost.

He finally fell asleep around two AM, still holding Amy's letter, and dreamt of lighthouses, locked boxes, and keys that opened them, and their hearts.

The dream started on a windswept cliff where an old lighthouse stood guard against the swirling darkness of the sea. Its beam swept across the water at regular intervals, each rotation revealing pieces of memory that floated like sea foam in the salty air. He found himself walking toward the tall structure, Amy's letter somehow turning into a brass key that grew warm in his hand with each step.

The lighthouse keeper's door was slightly open, creaking with each gust of sea wind. Inside, spiral stairs curled upward into darkness, but it wasn't the light above that caught his eye; it was the collection of locked boxes scattered around the circular room. Each box was unique: some carved from driftwood, smoothed by years of waves; others made of tarnished silver, reflecting distorted images of his face; and still others that seemed to be crafted from crystallized tears, catching and refracting the lighthouse beam into shards of pain and hope.

Amy appeared then, not as the woman who had written the letter of apology, but as she had been in those final days, her eyes rimmed with the red of sleepless nights and unshed tears, her hands trembling as they had when she'd tried to explain the files. She stood among the boxes like a curator in a museum, each container holding a different moment of their shared history that had curdled into resentment, hurt, disbelief, and anger.

"I tried to unlock them," she said, her voice echoing the distant lighthouse horn. "But the keys... they only work if you want them to."

He looked down at the key in his hand and realized with dreamlike logic that this wasn't just about opening boxes. Each lock symbolized a different emotion that had been stepped on in the past few weeks.

The first box he approached was the heaviest, carved from what looked like petrified heartwood. The key slid into the lock with surprising ease, and when the lid opened, instead of pain pouring out, there was... understanding. He saw her fear, her confusion, the way she'd been drowning in guilt at creating, then hiding, the files.

Box after box opened under his touch, each revelation softening the sharp edges of his anger. The lighthouse beam grew brighter, its rhythm syncing with his heartbeat as resentment dissolved into something more complex: a bittersweet acknowledgment of human fragility, of love that sometimes means letting go, and of forgiveness as an act of liberation rather than surrender.

When he reached the final box, Amy stood beside him, her face no longer marked by guilt but by something close to peace. Together, they turned the key, and inside was not a memory but a mirror reflecting both their faces, wearier, but somehow clearer. The lighthouse beam swept over them one last time, and he realized that forgiveness wasn't about forgetting or excusing, but about choosing to carry love instead of anger into whatever comes next.

He woke with salt on his cheeks and sunlight streaming through his bedroom window, Amy's actual letter still clenched in his hand, the paper soft from sleep and dreams. For the first time in three days, he reached for his phone with a clear heart, ready to write back.

Chapter 19
Amy - December 24th

Amy woke up at six in the morning, her heart already racing.

Christmas Eve. The gala. The presentation. The conversation with William would either fix everything or confirm it was permanently broken.

She showered, spent extra time on her hair, put on the dress she'd brought for the gala—deep green velvet that Dawn had helped her pick out weeks ago when everything still felt possible.

Dawn knocked at seven, let herself in, took one look at Amy, and smiled. "You look beautiful. And terrified. Perfect."

"I don't have a plan. I don't have talking points, a strategy, or any idea what I'm going to say."

"You're going to tell the truth. That's the plan."

"That's not a plan. That's just showing up and hoping."

"Welcome to how the rest of us live." Dawn handed her a coffee. "Drink this. You're meeting him in two hours, and you need to not pass out from anxiety."

Amy took the coffee and sat on the bed. "What if he doesn't forgive me?"

"Then he doesn't. And you'll survive. And you'll know you were brave enough to try."

"What if he does forgive me and I mess it up again?"

"Then you'll try again. That's how this works," Dawn sat beside her. "I'm going to find Jack before the gala, apologize to Lily, and tell him I'm staying for a while longer."

"Are you sure?"

"No. I'm terrified. But I'm doing it anyway." She squeezed Amy's hand. "We both are. Sisters being brave together."

"When did we become the kind of people who do terrifying things?"

"About three days ago, when we decided that being safe was worse than being scared."

They held hands until Amy's alarm went off at 8:30, signaling it was time to walk to the Bean Counter for coffee with William.

The walk to town felt longer than usual. Amy's heels clicked on the sidewalk, her heart hammering with each step, her mind racing through possible opening lines and discarding them all.

I'm sorry, it wasn't enough.

I love you was too much.

Thank you for meeting me. It was too formal.

She arrived at 8:55. William was already there, sitting at their usual corner table, with two coffees waiting.

He stood when he saw her. "Hi."

"Hi." She sat, wrapped her hands around the coffee cup for something to hold. "Thank you for this. For being willing to talk."

"I read your letter."

"I wasn't sure you would. I wasn't sure you'd want to."

"I read it three times," he said, looking down at his coffee. "You said you didn't fall for candidate number four. You fell for the man who made you forget numbers existed."

"That's true. That's the truth."

"I spent the last three days angry over the spreadsheet—about the clinical documentation, the compatibility metrics, and the decision point scheduled for the day we kissed." He looked up at her. "But I missed what you were actually saying. That you fell for me despite the plan. That the spreadsheet was fear, not strategy."

"It was both at first, but then it just turned into fear—fear that if I didn't have a backup plan, you'd see I was too much work and leave."

"Like your dad left."

She nodded, her throat tight. "My parents divorced when I was twelve. My mom said, she said if she'd been better, easier, less demanding, maybe he would've stayed. And I learned that love is conditional. That you have to earn it by being perfect."

"So you created a spreadsheet to ensure you could be good enough.

"I made a spreadsheet because organizing feels safer than feeling. Because if I could just control the variables, I could guarantee the outcome." She took a shaky breath. "But I can't control this. I can't control whether you forgive me or whether you trust me or whether you still want me after everything."

"I do want you. That's the problem. I'm still upset about the spreadsheet, and I still want you."

"I got rid of everything. All the backups. Every safety net. I'm showing up with just truth now."

"I know. Jack told me." William leaned across the table, stopping just short of touching her hand. "I forgive you. Not because what you did was okay. Not because the spreadsheet didn't hurt. But because I love you more than I love being right."

Her eyes filled with tears. "You love me?"

"I love you. Even angry. Even hurt. Even knowing you had seventeen other candidates and I was number four." He finally took her hand. "I love you because you're brilliant, stubborn, and brave enough to climb four hundred steps despite being terrified. I love you because you turn off alarms when you're trying to be present, you make terrible puns about organizational systems, and you love your sister even when she drives you crazy."

"William—"

"I love you because you're messy and complicated, and you try so hard to be perfect that you forget perfect isn't the point. Being real is the point. Being honest is the point. Being brave enough to show up anyway is the point."

She was crying openly now. "I love you too. I love you and I'm terrified and I don't know how to do this without a plan."

"We'll figure it out together. We'll be scared together. We'll mess up and apologize and try again." He squeezed her hand. "No spreadsheets. No cynicism. Just two imperfect people choosing each other."

"That sounds terrifying."

"It sounds perfect."

They sat there holding hands across the table, just looking at each other, both smiling, both choosing vulnerability over safety.

"We still have to present tonight," Amy said finally. "The whole town will be watching."

"We'll figure out what to say together. No scripts."

"No script feels dangerous."

"No script feels honest."

They finished their coffee, made plans to meet backstage at six-thirty to review, and walked out into the December morning feeling like maybe they'd figured out the key after all.

Amy spent the afternoon helping with last-minute gala preparations, but her mind was elsewhere—on William's words, on his forgiveness, and on the possibility that maybe they could actually make this work.

At five, she went back to the lodge to change. She found Dawn already in her dress, looking nervous and determined.

"I'm going to find Jack now," Dawn said. "Before the gala starts. Before I lose my nerve."

"Do you want me to come with you?"

"No. I need to do this alone. But will you walk with me to the community center?"

They walked together, both dressed for the gala, both trembling slightly, both about to do the bravest thing they had ever done.

At the community center, they saw Jack setting up chairs in the main hall. Lily was with him, wearing a red velvet dress and bouncing with excitement.

"There's Dawn. Dawn!" Lily shrieked, running toward them.

Dawn caught her, swung her up. "Hi, sweetheart."

"Daddy said you might not come. Are you staying for Christmas? Are you staying forever?"

Dawn set her down gently and knelt so they were eye level. "I'm sorry I made you sad. I'm sorry I said I was leaving. That was scary for you, wasn't it?"

Lily nodded, eyes wide.

"I was scared too, scared to stay, scared to be part of your family because I worried I might mess it up." Dawn's voice was trembling. "But I'm going to try anyway. I'm going to stay for a while longer, if your daddy still wants me to."

"He wants you to!" Lily hugged her. "He's been sad without you."

Jack moved forward slowly, and Amy noticed the hope and fear battling on his face. "Lily, go help Miss Amy with something, okay?"

Lily ran over to Amy and took her hand. They stepped back a little, making space for Dawn and Jack but staying close enough to see.

Dawn stood and faced Jack, her gaze meeting his without flinching. "I'm not leaving tonight. I'm scared, and I'll probably panic seventeen more times, but I'm staying for a while. I need to see if I can handle choosing you, Lily, this town, and this life. If you'll give me the chance to try."

"Are you sure?" His voice was cautious. Guarded. "Because I can't do this again. Can't watch you leave again. Lily can't handle that back and forth."

"I'm sure about the try," she clarified, her hands gripping her sides. "I've told the landlord to hold off on renting the Portland place for a month. I told the gallery I'd work the full spring season. I'm giving this a real shot, even though it absolutely terrifies me."

Jack pulled her close and kissed her. Not tentatively, not carefully, but fully and completely, as if he was choosing to believe her promise of a chance.

When they separated, Lily cheered. Amy wiped tears from her face, watching her sister take the first step toward bravery, watching Jack choose to believe in the possibility of her return.

It was possible—two scared people choosing each other and making it work despite their fears.

If Dawn could do it, maybe Amy could too.

Jack noticed Amy watching and smiled. "Thanks for lending us your sister."

"Thanks for being patient with her."

"Thanks for being patient with William," he countered. "He's been insufferable for three days."

"So has Amy," Dawn said, laughing.

They stood there together, Amy and Dawn, Jack and Lily, and for a moment it felt like family. Not the perfect, planned family Amy had always pictured. Just real people choosing each other.

"I need to find William," Amy said. "We have to prepare for the presentation."

"Good luck," Dawn said. "Be brave."

"You too."

Amy entered the community center, her heart pounding as she searched for William among the chaos of the final setup.

She couldn't find him anywhere, not at the stage, not in the main hall, not in the back rooms where volunteers were organizing last-minute details.

She asked Mayor Karen. "Have you seen William?"

"He's around somewhere, helping Bob with the lighting, I think," Karen looked at her directly. "Are you two okay? The whole town has been worried."

"We're working on it."

"Good. That's good," Karen's smile was genuine. "You're good together. The town could see it even when you two couldn't."

Amy found William twenty minutes later, backstage, adjusting the light rigging with Bob. He saw her, said something to Bob, and then climbed down.

"Hi," she said.

"Hi."

They stood there awkwardly, neither quite sure how to navigate this new territory of forgiveness, effort, and vulnerability.

"Nervous?" he asked.

"Terrified."

"Me too."

"I saw Dawn and Jack. She told him she's staying."

"That's good. Jack's been miserable."

"So has Dawn."

"So have we."

"Yeah."

The silence stretched between them, but it wasn't uncomfortable. Just nervous. Just two people who'd hurt each other trying to figure out how to start over.

Early guests began arriving. Amy could hear the murmur of voices, the excitement, and the anticipation of the evening's presentation.

"We should review what we're going to say," she said.

"We could. Or we could just wing it."

"Wing it. At a public presentation. In front of the entire town."

"We could tell them the truth. That we solved all the clues. That we found the final riddle. That the answer is surrender."

"And then?"

"And then we show them what surrender looks like."

Before she could respond, Mayor Karen appeared and grabbed both of them. "Five minutes to curtain! Do you have the solution to the Wish Box mystery? Please tell me you have it."

Amy looked at William. William looked at Amy.

"I think we do," Amy said softly.

"You think?" Karen's voice rose. "You don't know?"

"We know the clue," William said. "We're still figuring out what it means."

"Well, figure it out quickly! The whole town is counting on you!" She hurried off, leaving them alone in the backstage area.

"Did we just commit to presenting a solution we don't actually have?" Amy asked.

"We have the solution. We just don't know if it works yet."

"That's not reassuring."

"Nothing about this is reassuring."

They stood there as the crowd noise increased, as the five-minute warning turned into a two-minute warning, and as the moment approached when they'd have to walk on stage and present their findings to everyone.

"Together?" William said, offering his hand.

"Together," Amy agreed, taking it.

They walked toward the stage entrance, scared but hopeful, both deciding to show up anyway.

And Amy wondered if surrender actually meant that. Not giving up. Not quitting. Just having the courage to want something without any promise you'd get it.

Just showing up and hoping it was enough.

Chapter 20
William - December 24th

William stood in the wings with Amy's hand in his, both of them watching the crowd through the gap in the curtain. The community center was packed, every seat filled, people standing in the back, the whole town gathered to hear whether they'd solved the Wish Box mystery.

He took her hand, squeezed it. "I read your letter. The one you left at my shop."

She turned to him, breathless. "And?"

"And I forgive you. More than that, I understand. I was scared, too. We were both scared. We just chose different armor."

Her eyes filled with tears. "I deleted everything. Every backup. Every plan. I don't know what I'm doing anymore."

"Neither do I." He smiled, wiped a tear from her cheek. "Want to figure it out together?"

"Yes. God, yes."

They leaned toward each other, the kiss inevitable, necessary.

"You're on!" Mayor Karen's voice crackled through the backstage speaker. "Thirty seconds!"

They broke apart, both slightly breathless, both laughing at the terrible timing.

"We should—" Amy started.

"We should," William agreed.

They moved toward the stage entrance, and William suddenly understood something. The grand gesture he had been planning, the speech he had rehearsed, the thoughtful words he had arranged—all of it became insignificant.

Amy was about to walk on stage without a script. No plan. No safety net.

That was her surrender. That was her grand gesture.

She was showing up anyway.

Now it was his turn.

"Whatever happens out there," he said softly. "We're in this together."

"Together," she agreed.

The curtain was opened.

Amy

The spotlight struck Amy with the intensity of a physical force.

She walked onto the stage, William beside her, as the entire town came into view. Her parents sat in the third row, looking proud yet anxious. Dawn and Jack with Lily on Jack's shoulders, all of them smiling brightly. Mrs. Peterson in her usual seat, already dabbing her eyes. Mayor Karen standing near the stage, practically buzzing with excitement.

Hundreds of faces, all watching and waiting.

Amy took the microphone, her hand trembling slightly. William stood beside her, firm and attentive.

"Good evening," she said, her voice only slightly unsteady. "William and I have spent the last three weeks solving the clues that lead to the

Christmas Wish Box. We've searched through town history, followed riddles, and uncovered pieces of Holly Falls that we never knew existed."

She paused, looked at William. He nodded encouragement.

"We found seven clues altogether. The first led us to the town's founding site. The second pointed to the original well. The third through fifth took us through the chapel, the footbridge, and the market, each revealing part of the town's history and ourselves."

The crowd was listening attentively. Everything was going smoothly. She knew she could do this. Just stick to the facts, present the findings, and sit down.

Except that wasn't the truth.

"The sixth clue," she continued, "was hidden at the lighthouse. And the seventh, the final clue, was carved into the Wish Box itself. It said: 'The key is not to seek but to surrender.'"

She stopped. Took a breath. Made a choice.

"But that's not the real story."

William looked at her, surprise flickering across his face.

"The real story is that I came to Holly Falls with a plan. I had a spreadsheet. PROJECT: CHRISTMAS HUSBAND." She heard the gasps from the audience and pushed forward. "I thought I could organize my way to love. I thought if I was strategic enough, if I optimized for compatibility and minimized risk, I could control the outcome. I could guarantee I wouldn't end up alone."

The room had gone completely silent.

"So I made a list. Seventeen names. Men who seemed suitable. Men who checked boxes. And I put William on that list. Candidate number four."

She turned to look at him, saw his expression, a blend of surprise, pride, and love.

"I assessed him, made notes, and verified his qualifications through observation. I had a decision point scheduled for December 14th, the day we kissed on the lighthouse, to decide if he was worth keeping."

The crowd gasped. Someone murmured. Amy pushed forward.

"And when William found out, he looked at me like I was exactly what I was afraid of being, someone too broken to love, someone who treated people like projects instead of recognizing them as human beings. And you know what? He was right to be hurt because I did treat him like a project. At first."

Her voice cracked slightly. William moved closer, a silent show of support.

"But then I fell in love with him. Truly in love. The kind of love that makes spreadsheets pointless. The kind that's frightening because you can't control it. The kind that makes you want to delete every backup and show up without a plan, risking everything for a shot at something real."

She could see people crying now. Mrs. Peterson had her handkerchief in her hand. Her mother was holding her father's hand tightly.

"I realized something over the past few weeks. The spreadsheet wasn't about finding love; it was about avoiding it. About protecting myself from the risk of getting hurt. About controlling something that fundamentally can't be controlled."

She took a breath, forced herself to continue.

"I believed that if I planned everything perfectly, I couldn't fail. But the only way to fail at love is to never take the risk. And I nearly did that. I almost let my fear win. I almost let the need for control ruin the best thing that ever happened to me."

She turned fully toward William now, the audience forgotten.

"I don't have a plan anymore. I don't have a strategy, backup, or any idea of what I'm doing. I just have this: I love you. I love your lectures about cobblestones and the way you make me climb four hundred steps even though I'm terrified. I love your cynicism, which is really just protection, and your kindness that you try to hide. I love that you make me want to throw away every spreadsheet and just see what happens."

Her voice was shaking now, tears streaming down her face.

"I love you, and I'm scared, and I'm asking you, in front of everyone here, will you take a chance on someone who's still learning how to fall? Will you risk loving someone who might mess this up seventeen more times but promises to keep trying anyway?"

The silence was absolute.

William's face was unreadable.

Amy's heart was breaking.

She had done it. She had surrendered completely—publicly, vulnerably, with no safety net and no promise.

And now she just had to wait to see if it was enough.

William

William stepped forward and took the microphone from Amy's trembling hands.

He looked out at the crowd, at the entire town that had watched them fall for each other, that had rooted for them, and was now holding its collective breath.

"I need a minute," he said to the audience. Then to Amy: "Come with me."

Her eyes widened. "What?"

259

"Trust me." He took her hand, led her down the stage steps.

The crowd parted as he walked through, with Amy half-running to keep up, her heels clicking on the floor.

"William, where are we going?"

"You'll see."

He pushed through the community center doors into the December night. People followed; he could hear them and feel the crowd gathering behind him, but he didn't stop.

He led her down Main Street, toward the town square, toward the Wish Box that had started this whole thing.

When they arrived, the crowd had formed a circle around them. The entire town, it seemed, had followed them outside.

William turned to Amy, still holding her hand, and spoke loudly enough for everyone to hear.

"You want to know the solution? The final clue?"

She nodded, confused and hopeful and terrified.

"The key isn't to seek but to surrender. You don't unlock this box by being clever or strategic. You unlock it by having the courage to want something without knowing if you'll get it."

He let go of her hand. Dropped to one knee.

The crowd gasped. Amy's hands flew to her mouth.

"I came to this town three years ago convinced love was for fools and tourists," he said, looking up at her. "I built walls and called it wisdom. I stayed alone and called it safety. I protected myself from risk and called it being realistic."

"William—"

"Then you crashed into me on December first and ruined everything. You made me hope. You made me want. You made me believe that maybe the risk was worth it. Maybe the fall wouldn't kill me. Maybe being vulnerable was braver than being safe."

He could see she was crying, but she was also smiling.

"So here's my surrender: I love you. Spreadsheet and all. Every scared, controlling, brilliant part of you. I love that you color-code your life and turn off alarms when you're trying to be present. I love that you climb four hundred steps even though heights terrify you. I love that you're learning to be messy and real and brave."

"William—"

"Marry me," he said. "Not because it's on any schedule. Not because you fit any criteria. Not because you're candidate number anything. Marry me because I can't imagine my life without you in it. Because I want us to be scared together. Because I want to figure out what happens next with you. Because I love you more than I love being safe."

The crowd was completely silent. Waiting.

"Marry me, Amy Donovan."

She pulled him up, not letting him stay on his knee for a second longer. Her hands cupped his face, tears streaming down her cheeks.

"Yes," she said. "Yes. A thousand times yes."

She kissed him, and the crowd erupted.

Cheering, applause, and the sound of an entire town celebrating a love that was nearly lost and then found again.

When they broke apart, both of them crying and laughing, there was a sound behind them.

A click.

Mechanical, definite, clear.

They turned together.

The Wish Box was open.

The lid had released, the lock mechanism disengaged, and the ornate top lifted to reveal the interior that hadn't been seen in twenty-five years.

The crowd pressed closer, everyone trying to see.

Inside the box: a single piece of aged parchment, carefully preserved, and an antique key resting on a velvet cushion.

William reached in and carefully lifted out the parchment. Amy stood beside him, her hand on his arm, as he unfolded it.

The text was written in careful calligraphy, dated 1899, and signed by the founders of Holly Falls.

He read it aloud, his voice carrying across the silent square:

To those who prove themselves worthy,

Love is not found in the seeking,
Nor in the careful plan,
But in the brave surrender—
The trembling, open hand.

The greatest wishes aren't granted
By stars or fate or chance,
But chosen by the fearless
Who dare the lovers' dance.

What's won without the struggle
Has no weight, no worth, no cost,
But love that's earned through courage
Can never quite be lost.

So take this key, brave lovers,
Who faced your deepest fear,
And build a life together
Worth every fallen tear.

Love well, love brave, love honest,
Love through the doubt and pain,
For only those who surrender
True love will ever gain.

— The Holly Falls Founders, 1899

The silence that followed was reverent.

Then someone started clapping, followed by another person. Soon, the whole town was applauding, cheering, and celebrating.

Mayor Karen was crying openly. Mrs. Peterson was dabbing her eyes and saying, "I knew it, I knew it," to anyone who would listen. Amy's parents were hugging each other. Dawn and Jack were kissing, Lily sandwiched between them, demanding to know what was happening.

William carefully returned the parchment to the box, then pulled out the antique brass key. It was small, ornate, and had aged to a lovely patina.

"The key," Amy said, understanding. "The key to the box was always here. Inside the box itself."

"You can't find it through searching. You can only find it by having the courage to surrender."

"We did it," she said, laughing through tears. "We actually did it. We opened the Wish Box."

"We did." He pulled her close and placed the key in her hand. "This is yours. Our story. Our proof that surrender works."

"Our proof that love is worth the risk."

The crowd swarmed around them, hugging, congratulating, and touching the Wish Box as if it held real magic. Maybe it did. Maybe the magic was just the reminder that courage could unlock things that strategy never could.

William found himself shaking hands, accepting congratulations, and being pulled into hugs by townspeople who watched them fall apart and come back together.

Through it all, he held Amy's hand in his, kept her close, and kept choosing her again and again with every breath.

Dawn broke as Lily was in her arms, with Jack beside her. "That was the bravest thing I've ever seen," she said to Amy.

"I learned from watching you. You chose Jack. I chose William."

"We both chose to stop running."

"We both chose to surrender."

Jack patted William on the shoulder. "Welcome to the terrifying world of being loved by a Donovan sister."

"Wouldn't want to be anywhere else."

Lily wiggles down and runs to Amy. "Are you a princess now? You got the magic box open!"

Amy knelt and pulled her into a hug. "Not a princess. Just someone who was finally brave enough to want something."

"Can I be brave like you when I grow up?"

"You already are, sweetheart. You're the bravest person I know."

William watched Amy with Lily, Dawn with Jack, and the town celebrating around them while thinking about the poem in the Wish Box.

Love well, love brave, love honest, love through the doubt and pain.

That was the key. Not avoiding pain. Not preventing doubt. Not chasing perfection.

Just loving anyway. Bravely. Honestly. Through everything.

Mayor Karen appeared, still crying, holding a photographer. "We need photos! For the historical record! This is the first time in twenty-five years the Wish Box has been opened!"

They gathered around the box, with Amy and William in front and Mayor Karen beside them, as townspeople pressed in behind. The photographer kept snapping photos, capturing the moment when two scared people were brave enough to choose each other.

As the celebration carried on and people began drifting toward the community center for the gala dinner, William pulled Amy aside into a quiet corner of the square.

"Hi," he said.

"Hi." She was beaming. "We're engaged."

"We are."

"I don't have a ring."

"I don't need one. I just need you."

"That's very romantic."

"I'm trying." He pulled her close, rested his forehead against hers. "Thank you for being brave enough to surrender. For showing me what that looks like."

"Thank you for forgiving me. For loving me despite the spreadsheet."

"Because of the spreadsheet, it showed me exactly how scared you were and how much courage it took to choose me anyway."

They stood there in the December cold, surrounded by Christmas lights and celebration, and Amy thought about the journey that had brought them here.

From collision to collaboration. From spreadsheet to surrender. From carefully controlled to beautifully messy.

"I love you," she said. "No plan. No strategy. Just truth."

"I love you too," he said. "No cynicism. No protection. Just truth."

They kissed in the town square, in front of the now-open Wish Box, while Holly Falls celebrated around them. It was a town that believed in magic, legends, and the power of two scared people choosing bravery over safety.

The Wish Box had opened.

The legend was fulfilled.

And Amy Donovan, who had come to Holly Falls with a spreadsheet and seventeen candidates, was leaving with one man who made all her plans meaningless.

Not candidate number four. Just William. Just love. Just enough.

Epilogue
Amy - December 25th

Amy woke to the scent of pine, the warmth of William's chest against her back, and the dizzying awareness of a ring on her finger. Not the one she'd chosen, but one he'd slipped on her hand with shaking fingers and a whispered promise. "Temporary," he'd said, "until we pick one together." And somehow, that messy, unplanned promise felt like everything she'd never dared to wish for.

That she was engaged to William Crane, that she'd surrendered every plan and ended up exactly where she was supposed to be.

"You're thinking very loudly," William murmured against the back of her neck.

"I'm just processing. Yesterday was a lot."

"Yesterday was perfect."

"Yesterday I confessed to making a spreadsheet about you in front of the entire town."

"And I proposed in front of the entire town. We're even." He pulled her closer. "Merry Christmas."

"Merry Christmas." She turned in his arms and kissed him softly. "We're supposed to be at Jack's in an hour for breakfast."

"We have time."

They didn't rush. Got up slowly, made coffee together in William's small kitchen, moved around each other with the ease of people learning each other's rhythms. Amy borrowed one of his sweaters, too big but warm, and felt ridiculously happy about something as simple as putting it on.

By nine-thirty, they were walking to Jack's house, hand in hand, with the town peaceful and quiet on Christmas morning.

Jack's house was chaos in the best possible way.

Lily shrieked when she saw them and ran to hug Amy's legs. "You came! Daddy said you'd come, but I wasn't sure!"

"Of course we came." Amy knelt and hugged her properly. "We wouldn't miss Christmas with you."

Amy looked up and caught Dawn's eye across the room. Her sister smiled, happy but unsure, stealing glances at Jack with the cautious wariness of someone trying out new ground.

The house was full. Jack's parents, Amy's parents, Dawn helping in the kitchen, and Lily dragging everyone to see her presents. It was loud and messy, and nothing like the perfect, organized Christmas Amy had always imagined.

It was better. Amazingly better.

They gathered around the table, too many people for the space, chairs crowded too close together, conversations overlapping. Amy sat between William and her mother, watching the family she'd found rather than planned.

Her father is telling Jack's father a story from his Arizona days. Her mother and Jack's mother are comparing recipes. Dawn catches Jack's eye and looks away quickly, her cheeks flush with something between pleasure and panic. Lily was bouncing in her seat, too excited to eat properly.

"I have an announcement," Dawn said suddenly, standing. The table quieted. "I'm staying in Holly Falls. Permanently. I took the job at the art gallery downtown, and I'm moving into the apartment above the bakery next week."

Lily cheered. Jack reached for Dawn's hand, but she sat down quickly, deflecting his touch with a nervous laugh as the table erupted in congratulations.

Amy felt William's hand find hers under the table and squeeze gently.

This was the family she'd wanted. Not the perfect, organized, scheduled version from her spreadsheet fantasies. This messy, loud, imperfect collection of people who chose each other.

A single father and his daughter. A free-spirit sister learning to stay. A recovering cynic who'd learned to hope. A woman learning that being loved didn't require being perfect.

After breakfast, William pulled her aside into Jack's living room. "I have something for you."

He handed her a small wrapped box. Inside was an antique compass, brass and beautiful, with an inscription on the back: *For when you need direction, not a plan.*

Amy's eyes filled with tears. "It's perfect."

"You can still be organized. You can still make lists. You just don't have to let the plan control you anymore." He wiped her tears. "You can use this instead."

"Where did you find it?"

"I bought it last week. Before everything fell apart. I was going to give it to you at the gala, but then—"

"But then the spreadsheet destroyed everything."

"But then we chose each other anyway." He kissed her forehead. "That's better than any plan."

Amy pulled out her gift for him, wrapped last night in a panic after they'd left the gala. "I got you something too."

He unwrapped it carefully. A framed photograph of them at the lighthouse, taken by someone from the town paper. The back of the frame had an inscription she'd added: *The best things are unscheduled.*

William stared at it for a long moment, then pulled her close. "Marry me soon?" he whispered.

She laughed. "We just got engaged yesterday."

"So that's a yes to soon?"

"That's a 'let's figure it out as we go.'"

"I can work with that."

They rejoined the family, spent the morning opening presents and eating too much food, and watching Lily perform an elaborate puppet show she'd clearly been preparing for weeks.

It was messy and loud, and nothing went according to schedule.

It was perfect.

William

The town square was transformed for Christmas evening, with lights everywhere, carolers singing in front of the town hall, and families gathered around the tree for the traditional Christmas evening celebration.

William and Amy walked hand in hand, both bundled in coats and scarves, joining the crowd.

The Wish Box had been relocated. Mayor Karen placed it inside a display case at the town hall, where it was visible through the large front window. A plaque beneath it read: Opened Christmas Eve 2024 by Amy Donovan and William Crane, who proved that love requires surrender, not strategy.

"We're famous," Amy said, reading it.

"We're a legend."

"That's terrifying."

"That's Holly Falls."

They were stopped every few feet by townspeople wanting to congratulate them. Mrs. Peterson hugged them both and said, "I knew from the start you were meant for each other." Mr. Smithe offered free dinner at his restaurant for their rehearsal dinner. Mayor Karen was already planning their wedding, asking about dates, venues, and guest lists.

William fielded it all with patience, Amy beside him, both of them learning to accept that their love story now belonged to the town as much as to them.

They passed two teenage girls looking at the Wish Box through the window.

"Do you think it really grants wishes?" one asked.

"I think it just reminds you to be brave enough to make them come true yourself," the other answered.

William smiled. Exactly right.

Across the square, Dawn and Jack were dancing to the carolers' music, Lily sandwiched between them, all three of them smiling. Jack spun his daughter, and Dawn caught her, and William hoped he was watching a family forming right in front of his eyes, but knew it was too early to tell.

Not the traditional kind. Not the expected kind. Just the real kind.

Amy's mother appeared beside him. "Can I steal you for a moment?"

"Of course."

She led him a few steps away, then turned to face him directly. "Take care of my girl."

"I will. I promise."

"And let her take care of you. She needs to be needed, but for the right reasons now. Not because she's trying to earn love, but because she genuinely wants to give it."

"I understand."

"Good." She patted his arm. "Welcome to the family, William. We're glad Amy found you."

"I'm glad I found her, too."

He rejoined Amy and pulled her close as the carolers started "Silent Night." She rested her head on his shoulder, and they swayed softly to the music.

"Can I ask you something?" she said quietly.

"Anything."

"Do you want kids? Someday?"

He was quiet for a moment, thinking. "Someday. When we're ready. No timeline."

"I want them too. Not right away, but—" She looked up at him. "Maybe in a few years? When we've figured out the marriage thing first?"

"That sounds perfect." He kissed her forehead. "However it happens, whenever it happens, we'll figure it out together."

"Together," she agreed.

They stayed in the square as the evening deepened, as families drifted home, as the Christmas lights reflected off the snow. Holly Falls was peaceful, perfect, and exactly where they both belonged.

Amy

Later, they sat on the porch swing at the Evergreen Lodge, Amy, William, and Dawn, who'd appeared twenty minutes ago looking content and tired.

"We're getting there," Dawn said suddenly. "Getting where?" Amy asked. "You stopped running from control. I'm... still working on the commitment thing. But I stayed, didn't I? That's something."

"We're almost thirty. About time."

They laughed, the sound carrying across the quiet night.

"When you have kids," Dawn said, "I'm going to be the aunt who teaches them to break rules and have adventures and trust their instincts."

"If you and Jack ever... I mean, when you figure things out, I'll be the aunt who teaches them to plan ahead and make lists and think before they leap."

"They're going to be so confused."

"And so loved."

William's arm was around Amy, Dawn's head on Amy's shoulder, and for a moment, they just sat there, two sisters and the man Amy had fallen for, watching snow fall on Holly Falls.

Through the town hall window, Amy could see the Wish Box in its display case, lid open, legend fulfilled.

Three weeks ago, she'd come to this town with a spreadsheet and seventeen candidates and a desperate need to control every outcome.

Now she was sitting here with no plan at all. Just a fiancé who made her laugh, a sister who'd chosen to stay, a town that had embraced her, and a future that was completely uncertain.

She'd come looking for a husband.

She'd found something better: herself, a man who loved that self, and a family she didn't have to earn.

The wish hadn't been granted by magic. It had been granted by her courage to want it badly enough to risk everything.

And that, she thought, was the realest magic of all.

"What are you thinking?" William whispered.

Amy smiled. "That I have no idea what happens next."

"Good. Me neither."

"We still have to figure out so many things. Where we're going to live. What I'm doing about my job. When we're getting married. How we're—"

"We'll figure it out," he interrupted gently. "One decision at a time. Together."

"One decision at a time," she repeated, testing the words. They felt both terrifying and exactly right.

"Want to start now?" he asked.

"Start what?"

"Making decisions together. One at a time." He shifted slightly so he could see her face. "First decision: do you want to stay here tonight, or go back to my place?"

"That's easy. Your place. Your bed is more comfortable."

"Second decision: spring or summer wedding?"

"Summer. More time to plan without it being a plan." She smiled at the contradiction. "Third decision: are we doing this? Really doing this? Building a life together with no spreadsheets and no guarantees?"

"Yes," he said simply. "Every day. One decision at a time."

Dawn lifted her head and stood up with a yawn. "I'm going to leave you two alone to make your decisions. I have my own to make, like whether to stay up and help Jack build the new bookshelf he got Lily, or to go home to my own bed like a sensible person who isn't getting too attached."

"Choose the bookshelf," Amy said. "Choose him."

"I'm trying to. Some days are easier than others." Dawn's voice was soft, uncertain. "But I'm trying."

"Thank you for showing me that staying might be worth the risk."

Dawn left, and William pulled Amy closer, both of them watching the snow fall on the quiet town.

"You know what the strangest part is?" Amy said. "I don't miss the spreadsheet. I thought I would. I thought I'd feel lost without the structure. But I don't."

"What do you feel?"

"Free. Terrified. Happy. Like I'm exactly where I'm supposed to be, even though I have no idea where I'm going."

"That's called living, Amy. Welcome to it."

She laughed, leaned in, and kissed him softly but confidently. When they parted, her voice trembled with conviction. "I love you. Even if I don't have a blueprint for it."

"I love you too. We'll figure it out together."

"One decision at a time."

"One decision at a time."

They sat there as the clock tower struck midnight, marking the transition from Christmas Day to the next, with the future stretched out before them, uncertain, unplanned, and full of possibility.

Amy Donovan had deleted her spreadsheet.

She'd opened her heart.

The Wish Box had opened, too.

And in the end, they were all the same kind of magic, the courage to want something without knowing if you'd get it, and the grace to build it one brave decision at a time.

Together.

Hello!

My name is Judy Powers, and I have been crafting stories for years, but only recently decided to share them with the world. I specialize in sweet romance where love finds a way, and every character is someone you'd want to know.

When I'm not writing, I'm an empty nester living with my husband and three cats. You might also find my husband on the front porch, offering treats to the local squirrels who've learned exactly where to get a snack!